THE MESSENGER

What is wrong with the house next door? When Rose's parents buy it, to turn into an annexe for the Wood Briar Hotel, they brighten it with cheerful colours and pretty patterns. But the house has a terrible effect on people, filling them with a sense of tragedy and despair. What is the secret of the deep, dark cupboard with its strange smell of the sea? What horror from the past casts its shadow upon the living?

When Rose becomes thirteen – 'that special age' as the surprising Mr Vingo puts it, 'when your mind and spirit are aroused to a state of tempestuous movement' – she is chosen to be a messenger of the Great Grey Horse.

Noble, beautiful and brave, the horse was long ago the favourite charger of the vile Lord of the Moor, and his heroism in the face of treachery saved a whole village. Now he lives on, with a mission to protect innocent people from evil, misery and violence.

A tune played on Mr Vingo's marmalade-coloured piano summons Rose to the horse, and she is galloped back through time into the heart of the mystery. Can she meet the horse's challenge? Can she find a way to break the spell of tragedy? As the horse's messenger she must not fail . . .

This is the first book about Rose and the Great Grey Horse. In the second book, BALLAD OF FAVOUR, the horse takes Rose to a dilapidated old house in a seedy part of town, where a small child cries in helpless terror . . .

ABOUT THE AUTHOR

MONICA DICKENS, a great-granddaughter of Charles Dickens, went to St. Paul's School for Girls, in London, where she won two scholarships but was expelled for feeding her school hat to the family dog.

Since then she has become famous all over the world for her bestselling books. As well as nearly thirty adult titles, she has written a number of stories for children, including the *Follyfoot* books (which were made into a very successful TV series) and four *World's End* titles.

Many of her books reflect her lifetime love of animals, especially horses – in fact, animals are such a part of her life that she finds it hard to keep them out of her stories. In the *Messenger* series she writes about the kind of horse one might dream about: wild, majestic and beautiful.

Monica has two grown-up daughters, a horse called Robin, two dogs, Mollie and Rosie, and an assortment of cats.

Monica Dickens

The Messenger

Illustrations by
Glynis Overton

The Messenger was published in the U.K. in 1985
in hardback by William Collins Sons & Co. Ltd.,
and in paperback in Armada,
by Fontana Paperbacks, 8 Grafton Street, London W1X 3LA.

A division of the Collins Publishing Group.

© Monica Dickens 1985

Printed in Great Britain by
William Collins Sons & Co. Ltd., Glasgow.

CHAPTER ONE

Rose had always thought of herself as a rather humdrum, matter-of-fact kind of girl, to whom nothing extraordinary had ever happened, and perhaps never would. So what did happen that afternoon in the kitchen when the newspaper caught fire was totally odd and unexpected.

Rose's parents, Philip and Mollie Wood, owned a small hotel near the sea, three miles away from Newcome, a busy coastal town. Rose was working in the kitchen that Saturday afternoon, chopping vegetables for soup, while Hilda, one of the helpers who came and went, read a folded newspaper while she stirred custard.

Hilda always read her favourite newspaper while she was cooking or washing up or mopping the floor, holding up close to her one good eye its dreadful news of murder and car crashes and scandal among film stars.

'Custard's burning!' When Rose yelled at her, Hilda lowered the newspaper to swivel her eye into the saucepan, and the edge of the paper caught and flared – a conflagration on the stove.

Hilda shrieked and dropped the custard spoon on the floor and stepped backwards into the cat dish. Rose pounced forward, turned off the gas and, without thinking, brought her hand down on the burning newspaper. The flames dwindled immediately, and went out.

Shaking and terrified at what she had done, Rose took her hand off the charred paper, expecting to see all the skin gone from her palm.

'What happened?' Her mother was there, fresh pink cheeks gone white with fright. 'Oh, your hand! Oh . . .'

5

'It's all right.' Rose stared at the palm of her hand, smooth, not even red, the head line, the heart line, the deeper line curving round the base of her thumb, which Mrs Ardis the chambermaid said was the line of your death, perfectly whole and unscarred. There was no pain. The fire was out.

Her mother put the burned saucepan into the sink. Hilda set off to Newcome Hollow village to buy another newspaper. Rose's father came in to tell them, 'Something's burning.'

'The whole kitchen would have burned, Phil, but this brave girl saved us.'

Rose beamed and hung her head. 'It was nothing.'

'It was a miracle. I saw it as I came through the door. The whole stove was in flames.' Rose's mother's round blue eyes were huge with exaggeration. 'She put her hand on it and it went out – without even burning her.'

'She's in shock, Mollie. That's why there's no pain.'

'No, look.' Rose showed him her miraculous hand.

'Hrhm.' Philip Wood cleared his throat, a sign that he was going to explain. 'Something in the way she cupped her hand made a vacuum that instantly eliminated all the carbonizing oxygen.' He had a logical, scientific mind, and could explain anything away, even fairy tales and true ghost stories.

Rose went back to chopping vegetables in an ordinary way. But that evening when she was sitting close in front of the television set in the upstairs lounge, nodding over a boring talk show, she sat up with a shock when one of the talkers turned and smiled right out of the screen at her and said, 'Wake up, Rose, this is important.'

'What is?'

'Be quiet,' one of the twin Miss Mumfords snapped. 'We can't hear.'

'Did you hear what that man said to me – the one with the beard?' Rose turned round to where the elderly twin sisters sat on the sofa, with their skirts pulled down over their neat knees, like dolls.

'I can't hear anything when you keep chattering.'

'This is only meant for you Rose, anyway,' she thought the man said, but when she turned back to him his shaggy head was fading into a commercial, the smile fading last, teeth very white and lips very pink in the hole in his beard.

At the end of the commercials there was a different person talking on the screen.

'Where's the man with the beard?' she asked the text book salesman, a one-nighter who was also in the hotel lounge.

'What man?'

Had Rose imagined him? What was going on? What was it that was only meant for her? Two weird things in one day. What was happening to her?

Rose was almost thirteen. She had lived here for four years, since her mother had plunged into the hotel business to try to add some money to Philip Wood's salary as a tester for a consumer magazine, which told its readers things like what make of washing machine worked best.

It looked less like a hotel than a large, odd-shaped and rather ugly house, which is what it used to be. It was built about 1900 when they favoured gables and pinnacles and cowled chimneys and odd little balconies, and a stained glass window half way up the staircase that threw blue and yellow sun diamonds on to the dark red carpet.

It was not like a hotel, with rooms opening off straight corridors. Some of the bedroom doors were in unexpected places, opening awkwardly the wrong way, so that they hit a bannister post or the big double doors of the linen cupboard on the landing. None of the rooms was quite square, and some of them were reached by two or three stairs up or down. The bathrooms had been fitted in wherever the plumbers could put pipes, not where you would expect them. New guests were sometimes found in dressing-gowns, wandering, lost, far off the trail.

The dining-room led on to a wide front verandah, with a view across the road of the billowing sand dunes that lay between the hotel and the beach. Round the corner at the side, there was another little odd-shaped verandah, dark and draughty, with a sagging roof over which was balanced a narrow round turret room. Rose had always liked this room, because it had curved walls and windows and a floor that sloped towards the middle so that furniture legs had to be propped. But guests found it too small and dark and uncomfortable, and it was only used when the hotel was full.

Fifteen guests was the limit, with a few more if they were toddlers who could sleep on sofa cushions on the floor, or babies who slept in car cots, or sometimes in a bottom drawer.

'Don't shut the drawer!' Rose, coming back from getting a snack while she was babysitting for guests who had gone shopping, had once found Mrs Ardis the chambermaid just about to shut in and suffocate the Robinson's baby with a push of her grey gym shoe.

When Rose's mother Mollie took over the small hotel, it was called 'The Cavendish', which was pointless and much too grand. Mollie, who was a romantic, called it 'Wood Briar Hotel', because the girl who lived there was Rose Wood. Philip Wood called it a glorified boarding house.

Rose worked for her mother at weekends and in the holidays, cooking, cleaning, making beds, and being a waitress in a short blue and white check apron that tied in a bow at the back and looked odd in the summer over shorts.

Most of the money she made was spent at a stable a few miles from the hotel, where she was learning to ride.

She was not learning very much. The classes were not

8

exciting – walk, trot and sometimes canter, if you could make your horse canter – and Rose seemed to be the worst in the class. Some days, she just bumped about, or fell off even at a trot. The horse they gave her, a pale, bony animal called Moonlight, which her father called The Mule, would almost never canter, except once when she was allowed to go out with a group on the moor, and Moonlight had suddenly turned and lumbered off for home, going right into the stable, where he would have brained Rose against the top of the door if she had not been lying on his neck, clutching his thin mane and praying.

Rose loved going to the stable, because of the horses. Even though she was a clumsy, hopeless rider who could fall off at a standstill if necessary, she was fascinated by all the horse smells, and by the sounds of a creaking saddle, the clink of a bit, the reverberating rumble of a long snort blown into the wind, the lid of the wooden oat bin, the stamp of a shod foot, the thrilling dull pounding of hoofs when they were out on the turf of the moor, the slosh of mud at a gateway, the crisp greed of Moonlight, stoking himself with hay.

After riding, when she had cleaned out his pungent stable and brushed as much of his bony frame as she could reach, she would lean over his stable door to breathe in the strong-flavoured scents that called her to some emotion she could not name, before she dragged herself away back to the hotel to wash the horse smell off her hands with regret, and serve teas.

This Sunday, after the miracle of the fire, and the bearded man on television, Rose went to the stable with greater hope. When she got her bicycle out of the shed behind the hotel and pushed it through the long grass beyond the lawn, interwoven with tall spring flowers that her mother never wanted to have mown down, there was this new hope that now that something rather extraordinary

9

had happened to her at last, she might suddenly be able to ride well. Moonlight might transform himself into the horse of her dreams, who she had always imagined came from the stars, pawing and arching his neck outside her window at night, if only she could see him.

Beyond the gate at the end of the back garden, she rode the bicycle along the path through the small wood, bumping over roots, swerving for a low branch, splashing through a puddle, wearing her riding hat, making the old small bicycle into a horse. This summer, she had planned to save part of her wages for a new bicycle, but if she turned into someone who could really ride, and they let her ride other horses, like Mr Pepper and Red Admiral who went to horse shows, she would spend it all on horses.

Where the narrow woodland path opened out to the light and clouds and blowing grass of the beginning of the moor, Rose pulled the left rein and yanked the bicycle on to the wider gravel track and out on the road that led to the stables.

Would they see her as different? At the hotel, she was something of a heroine for having marvellously put out the fire, which would have sent the whole gabled and turreted edifice up in flames. (The story improved each time it was told.) Would they be impressed? If she showed Mrs Benson or Joyce her unharmed hand and told them about the fire, would they say, 'Admiral for you today!' and give her a leg-up?

No, they would not. They saw her as plain old Rose, who had not washed her jodhpurs or cleaned her boots and, because two people had come in late for the hotel lunch, was not in time to go out on the ride, and would have to slog round the muddy ring with the duffers.

'And clean Moonlight off before you tack him up. He's laid down again.'

Brown horses, on whom it doesn't show, always lie down

10

in clean straw. Moonlight, being a pallid cream colour with pink eyelids and nose, always lay down in manure.

But today, Moonlight cantered one and a half times round the ring, and Joyce shouted, 'All *right*!' in her encouraging riding teacher voice; not the bad mood one that roared, 'Oh my *God*!' or, 'Hold him *up*, dammit, he's going as if he had five legs!'

Rose spun home along the road from the stables, feeling like a jockey, because her knees came up high on the small bicycle. The dark little wood was ahead of her, and before it, off to the left, the first shoulder of the moor, dark blue in the afternoon shadow, and farther off the higher ground, greening in the spring, where the sheep were.

Lambing time was just over. The little ones would be in the pasture, trying out the bounce of their legs, while their mothers steadily tore at the grass, to manufacture milk.

Rose looked at the watch her father had given her, 'Hrhm – in the hope that you may be on time for anything except your meals.' Just time to turn up towards the moor and see if the ewes and lambs were still near the farm. In the wood, instead of taking the path home, she turned left and rode to the edge of the trees, then flung down her bike and ran uphill through the bushes to where she could climb on the wall and look into the broad sheep pasture and over the farther wall to the wider, wilder part of the moor.

She was singing. She usually sang in her head while she rode, to keep the rhythm of Moonlight's slovenly walk and unwilling trot, and she always sang to him under her breath when she brushed him down. She was still singing now, not out loud with words, but a tune in her head that she did not recognize. Where had she heard it? The air of the moor seemed to pick it up, and there was a drift of words that were not quite words, and the tune rose up joyfully in her head and then dropped into a sort of quick

11

He posed for a moment . . .

rumbling on the same note, like a – like a what? Like the snort of a horse? Was someone riding on the other side of the hill?

As she listened, she heard the drum beat of galloping hoofs, far away at first, but coming closer so fast that she knew the horse must be flying over the moor at a tremendous rate of speed. And then she saw him. A big grey riderless horse with a long mane and tail, streaking beyond a line of trees – sun, shadow, sun – the most beautiful horse she had ever seen.

At the end of the trees, he suddenly stopped, forelegs stiff, head up. He posed for a moment, then shook his handsome head, bucked, and was gone.

Down below in the pasture there were sheep and lambs, but Rose was not looking at them. The sight of the splendid horse had moved her to a pitch of excitement. She wanted to follow him, to run crazily over the moor, looking for his hoof tracks. Yet the thrill was mixed with fear, a dread of something unknown that made her shiver, although she was not cold.

'Hrhm.' Her father's remembered voice brought her back to earth. 'In the hope that you may be on time . . .' She looked at her watch and hurled herself off the wall and back down through the bushes. She bumped her bicycle along the path, bawling loudly, 'Onward, Christian so-ho-ho-holdyahs!', threw the bike in the grass, kicked off her muddy boots, crashed through the back door, tied a kitchen apron over her riding clothes and began to cut crusts off the big rectangular loaf to make toast.

CHAPTER TWO

The elderly twin Miss Mumfords had been at the hotel all winter, because their own house in town was too cold. 'Not that Wood Briar is an oven,' they said, shaking their heads, one of them in a negative way, the other, because her head always shook slightly, negative or positive.

There were always a few winter regulars, as well as the salesmen passing through, and odd people visiting the hospital or the university in Newcome. Sometimes pale people would come to convalesce after an illness, although the winters here were harsh, and the winds that blew over the sand dunes from the long open beach and Sandy Neck smacked the hotel full in the face and moaned in the drain pipes, and had once broken one of the glass dining-room doors all over a man eating bacon and scrambled eggs.

Now the Miss Mumfords were moving out, unregretted, because they were boring and critical and found mean little ways to try to reduce their bill, and the summer people would soon be coming in. Dozens of them. Some stayed a week or two, and some came back every year, like Ben's family. What would Ben be like this summer? At fifteen, he would probably notice Rose even less than last year. Travelling people came for a night or two, attracted by the beach, foreigners on tours, Americans, who are less foreign because you can usually understand what they say.

In July and August, Rose's short strong back ached from carrying baskets of laundry and making up clean beds, day after day.

This year, there would be even more, because Mollie Wood had bought the smaller house next door after the old gentleman died there, and it was to be Wood Briar Annexe, with three extra bedrooms.

'And all those towels and sheets to carry across the garden, *gracias muchas*.' Rosita's 'Thank you very much' meant 'No, thank you', with a toss of the hair and a roll of the fiery eyes that threatened one Spanish chambermaid walking out before the summer even began.

'The painters will be finished tomorrow,' Mollie told everyone after supper. Rose and her parents usually stayed in their own rooms at the back of the hotel, but this was the Mumfords' last night, and the sick man and his nurse would be leaving soon, so there was wine and gingerbread in the lounge. 'Shall we start getting the annexe ready, Rose? The curtains and bedspreads came – scarlet and gold chrysanthemums, the pattern you wanted. It's going to be beautiful.'

'Take more than a few red and yellow mums to beautify that old place,' one Miss Mumford said, looking suspiciously into her wine glass for flies before sipping at it, and making a face. 'It's a misfit. Always was.'

'Only because it was so dark before we redecorated, with those heavy curtains and the panelling.'

'My sister and I,' Miss Mumford continued sombrely, 'went to a birthday party there when we were children.'

'Dressed alike?' Rose asked.

She was genuinely interested in the idea of two identical little Mumfords in white dresses with blue sashes and hair ribbons, pretending to be each other, to fool the grown-ups; but Miss Mumford said, 'That's not for you to ask, nor me to tell you.'

'I only *asked*!' Rose felt a hot surge of fury at the silly, secretive old woman who had never done anything in her life worth being secretive about, and her father said, 'Rose!' in rebuke and her mother cried, 'Rose!' in amazement. Rose was known for being amiable and patient. It wasn't like her to fire up and scowl and hang her hair forward and hiss under it something that sounded like, 'Gee!', or even 'Jeeze!'

The sick man yawned and closed his eyes.

'I've never forgotten that party,' said the other Miss Mumford with the shaky head, who had once been married, but had changed her name back to Mumford when her husband died of drink. 'My sister was frightened by some kind of animal in the garden. A mad bull, she said, though no one believed her. And then they played hide and seek.' Her slipped face with the moles and faded, anxious eyes pouted childishly. 'I cried and cried and our mother had to take us home.'

'Why did you cry?' Rose was sitting on the floor with her back to the television. Even though the sound was turned down, just the picture jabbering silently, because the sick man's nurse could not exist without it, she was not going to risk that man with the beard suddenly coming after her again.

'How should I know?' shaky-head rebuked her. 'I was frightened.'

'What of?' Rose looked up, her anger quickly replaced by curiosity.

'Same thing that frightened the old lady. You could hear her throw up the window and scream for help. You could hear it from the village, they said.'

'Hear what?' The sick man woke up.

'Her blood-curdling screams, dear.' Miss Mumford quite liked the sick man, because he was powerless.

'Oh, what nonsense,' Rose's mother said cheerfully. 'I never heard a thing.'

'That was all before your day. By the time you took over this hotel and changed everything round so no one could find anything, she was dying.'

'He drove her to it. No one ever saw the old man after

that, till he was carried out feet first,' the other sister said. 'The night he died – good riddance to him – there was a great thunderstorm. There's people in the village who swear they heard the thunder of the devil's hoofs, come to take him away, and saw in a streak of lightning the white flash of the dead man's spirit.'

Philip Wood laughed, and Mollie said, 'I don't remember a storm that night.'

'I'm only telling you what I heard.' Miss Mumford lowered her eyes.

'Go on,' Rose urged, but Miss Mumford pursed her lips as if there were a drawstring round them, and the other sister started to complain about the old man's family.

'Never. bothered much about him, but those so-called daughters of his and that son from heaven-knows-where soon turned up once he'd gone, to see what they could get out of it.'

'There were a lot of children who came with them when they packed up,' Rose's mother remembered. 'I was surprised the family didn't want to keep the house as a summer place.'

The Miss Mumfords made blank eyes and sipped their wine like birds at a drinking fountain, and said no more.

Next day, it was a relief to find them gone when Rose got back from school. They were a dead weight. Mrs Ardis, who pretended to be psychic to show that being a chambermaid was beneath her, had burned some sweet herbs in the grate behind the electric fire in their room, to get rid of the sour vibrations.

Now the summer could begin.

But it was still cold, with a driving rain, and the wind picking up off the sea. Rose and her mother put mackintoshes over their heads like capes and ran with the bedding and curtains across their back garden, through the gap they had made in the fence, and in through the back door of the annexe.

The painters were just clearing up. The gloomy old kitchen had been converted into a little snack kitchen, with the rusty stove and low sink replaced by neat new fittings and a table and chairs, so that guests could keep food in the refrigerator and make their own breakfast and sandwiches.

'Wrong, right there for a start,' Philip Wood had warned his wife. 'Meals are where your good money is. People have got to come to the dining-room.'

'But sometimes it's so nice not to have to. Remember when we were in that dear little Italian villa . . .'

'Mosquitoes and tummy aches.' He would not be romantic. 'Get 'em into the dining-room for meals.'

' . . . I want people to be happy.'

She did. She wanted the painters to be happy with the beautiful job they had done. The bedroom walls were pale yellow, to make the house look sunnier, and the doors and woodwork were shining white. The dark panelled cupboards in the kitchen had been painted a brighter yellow, with orange knobs.

But the head painter was not completely happy. 'Three coats of marigold yellow, that wood panelling took, and it still dried up dingy. That's a fourth coat it's just had – keep your fingers off it, Rose! Let me know if it don't dry right.'

'Oh, it will.'

'And about that stain on the floor tiles.'

'I did that.' Rose had dropped a tin of orange paint when she was helping with the knobs.

'Can't seem to get it off, even with the wire brush.'

'We'll keep trying. We can always put an orange mat over it.' Rose's mother wanted perfection so badly that she could make something seem perfect, even if it wasn't.

In the large front bedroom on the ground floor, they hung the colourful new curtains at the bay window and put the matching cover on the cushion of the narrow window seat. Rose had known as soon as she looked at the fabric

18

catalogue that this was it. The flowers had yelled at her off the page: 'Us!'

The chrysanthemums were gorgeous shaggy splashes of scarlet and gold, all looking upwards, with climbing stems and ivy leaves and red berries, botanically insane, but a delight for the eyes of people who would wake in the big double bed, and realize that they were on holiday and did not have to get up.

While they were making the bed, Rose jumped forward to pat out a crease in the middle, and thumped back on the floor so hard that the door of the cupboard in the wall opened.

She kicked it shut – 'Watch the paint!' – but when she turned round to get the pillows, the door had swung open again.

It was a very deep cupboard with shelves at the sides and a rail at the back, almost like a little room. Three or four people could go right into it and shut the door without suffocating. The painters had done it yellow also, but it was still dark at the back where it turned sideways into a space for suitcases.

Rose went inside to check the handle from that side, shut the door and had a moment of panic in the dark when the handle would not turn.

'It's locked!'

It seemed like an eternity before the door opened on her mother's calmly smiling face. Rose pushed the door shut again and leaned on it, but the door leaned back and opened again as soon as she was across the room.

'It's an old house. The floor is crooked.' Mollie took one of the wooden wedges that were in the windows to stop them rattling when the wind blew in from the sea, and pushed the thin edge tightly under the door. They laid the new bedspread on the bed like a ceremonial vestment, and Rose kicked off her shoes and jumped up to lie full length on it for a blissful moment, inhaling the fresh paint and crisp new fabric.

19

CHAPTER THREE

Next day, the weather was worse. Rose and her friend Hazel rode home from school together as far as the village, heads down and shoulders hunched aganst the rain. At the corner of her street, Hazel, who hated emotion, fished a wet plastic package out of her bicycle basket and thrust it at Rose, and was blown away up the street by the wind in her rain cape like a spinnaker.

The hotel lay at the end of a row of houses outside Newcome Hollow village on an open road where the driving rain, salty from the sea, pushed Rose sideways and plastered her hair into her right eye.

Her mother leaned out of a window and shouted, 'Come in by the front door!' Rose never did, but anything could happen on a birthday. She dropped her bike under a bush, and as she ran up the wooden steps and opened the door, she saw a gigantic silver 13 hanging from the ceiling light in the middle of the hall.

'Congratulations!' Two salesmen and the sick man and an American couple looking for the English spring all smiled and praised Rose, as if she had done something clever. Even the sick man managed a slack smile from deep in his chair, and gave her five pounds.

Mollie was giving the guests a buffet supper so that Rose would not have to be a waitress tonight, but before she dressed for the family dinner in their own rooms upstairs at the back of the hotel, Rose ran across the garden and the neglected orchard next door to feast her eyes once more on the elegant bedroom with the chrysanthemum curtains and spread.

How quickly the smell of fresh paint and new fabric can fade! No one would ever know its tantalizing pristine aroma of yesterday. Two days of rain had made the room smell damp. The unwedged window was rattling in the gale. The cupboard was open again. The wedge was out on the floor. As Rose went round the bed to shut the door, she moved through a draught of cold air that must come from the loose window.

Before she shut the infuriating door, she made herself look into the deep cupboard, and saw that there was already a small patch of damp on one of the yellow walls between the shelves. The cupboard smelled musty, like old shoes, with a faint trace of that rotting sea smell that you got when you went under the pier at low tide for mussels.

Rose left the cupboard open to air it out, put the wedge in the rattling window, shrugged a shoulder against the draught that was still in that spot, and went through the kitchen to the back door. The painter was right. The marigold paint did dry to more of an ochre. Orange curtains were needed at the small window over the sink. She climbed on to the draining board to measure the length with her arm, and, stepping down, knocked two of the new yellow pottery cups on to the floor. Rose was used to breaking things. In the hotel kitchen or the pantry, nobody even looked round at the sound of breaking glass or china; but, unaccountably, the two smashed cups sent her into a storm of weeping.

I'm so stupid. She was plunged into sadness.

Sad on your birthday? Was this what growing up was – minding about silly mistakes? Shut up, Rose. She shook herself like a dog, picked up the pieces, wiped her eyes and nose on the painters' dirty roller towel and galloped away through the long wet grass shouting, 'I'm thirteen! I'm grown up!'

'Not quite.' Her father, home from the laboratory, was

She made herself look into the cupboard . . .

coming from the garage. 'But you're in your teens at last.' He gave her one of his stiff hugs, which she had had to teach him, since his mother had never hugged him.

'I was in my teens three years ago, Dad.'

'Not officially, until the actual word teen is in your age.'

Philip Wood was a perfectionist too, but it had actually to *be* so. He couldn't make it seem so, like Mollie.

'Now that I'm in my teens,' Rose said at supper, 'I'm going to call you Mollie and Phil.'

'I don't see why not.' Rose's mother was only thirty-three, and looked younger.

'I do.' Her father was at his nicest tonight, quite funny and fatherly in his dry, tied-in-knots way. 'I think I probably forbid it.'

'Oh, Phil.' Mollie laughed and winked at Rose. 'It's only a joke.'

'Is it, Rose?'

'I don't know. A lot of people at school call their parents by their first names, especially the divorced fathers. "I'm going to stay with generous George," they'll say. Or, "I heard Robert and my mother talking about me on the extension phone.".

Her father gave four good reasons why this was a mistake: breakdown of nuclear family, child's loss of parent figure, parent's loss of responsibility, fallacy of the equality principle proved in various civilizations, etc., etc.

Rose fidgeted and ate the last of the fried potatoes.

Mollie went out to get the cake, and before they lit the candles they took it to the upstairs lounge to share with the guests.

Rose had her hand on the switch to turn off the lights before her mother came in with the cake, but before she touched the switch, all the lights in the lounge went out by themselves.

'Line must have come down in the wind.' Mollie came in

with the cake and birthday candles. 'The only light in the hotel.'

As Rose blew them out, and everyone applauded in darkness, there was a crash from below and a scream, and then a loud banging and some shouts.

Cigarette lighters were lit. Mollie found candles. Philip went for the big torch.

In the hall, Jim Fisher, who was working in the kitchen this week, had dropped a tray of coffee cups. The front door was open, and a large person in a wet coat like a seal had blown in with the wind and rain.

Everybody came down the stairs with candles and cigarette lighters. Someone went to shut the door against the wind. 'Nice evening,' the large man said from the shadows. He breathed heavily, as if he had been running. 'I'd like a room, please.'

'For the night?' Phil came through the back of the house behind the wide beam of the torch, and ran it up and down the man, like a policeman.

The man laughed, for some reason, and then coughed and wheezed and finally said: 'And the next, and the next, and the next.'

Rose's father told Jim to get the luggage from the car, but the man said, 'No car. No luggage. It's here.' He dropped a soft, bulky bag on the floor.'

'You come in a cab?'

'I got a lift a mile from the station.'

'Hitching in this storm?' the American man asked.

'A very nice lady. She couldn't see a thing.'

Lights came on suddenly. The man stepped forward and made a small bow towards Rose on the stairs. His dark grey coat looked as if it had shrunk on him in the rain. His small hat was turned up in the front over a wide wet slab of face.

'So this is the lady who is thirteen.' He said it as if he were expecting it as a known fact, not something just discovered when the light came on, and the silver 13 was hanging there.

'This is my daughter Rose,' her father said, rather stiffly.

'Rose of all roses,' the man intoned in a high, quoting voice, 'Rose of all the world. A birthday present for you,' he said, but he did not give her anything.

His name was Mr Vingo. First name? When Mollie had asked him this for the hotel register, he lowered his head and wheezed a bit and mumbled something that might have been Harvey, but wasn't, so Mollie wrote 'R. V. Vingo.'

He lived in the Mumfords' room for two days. Then, as the clouds raced away and the sun came out in sudden steamy warmth, a lorry arrived and unloaded two suitcases for him and a small yellow upright piano on to the gravel car park at the side of the house.

Mr R. V. Vingo was a composer. He was in the process of setting a long poetic legend to music. When his sister's husband came home from abroad and threw Mr Vingo out, he had come here from London through the storm to stay and work.

'How did you know about us?' Rose asked.

'I heard.'

'We're famous.' Rose's mother smiled complacently.

Rose had meant, 'How did you know that this would be the kind of place that would let you bring a little old piano with yellow keys and curly iron candle holders, and would have a turret room stuck off on its own where you could play without bothering anyone?'

'That floor won't hold,' Philip Wood said when he came home and heard that Mr Vingo had moved into the round turret room.

'Yes it will,' Mollie said. 'I asked the carpenter to look at the joists there when he was working in the annexe. It's only the porch ceiling that sags. There's a big space in between.'

Nevertheless, after a few days, Dr Alice Pomeroy, who was here for her annual week of testing students in anatomy and physiology at the hospital nursing school, gathered up her working papers from the side verandah, from which she could hear Mr Vingo's incessant piano, going over and over the same phrases, as composers do. 'Sometimes he sings.' She shook her head regretfully and took her papers into the small back lounge in the empty annexe, which had been the old gentleman's study. On Friday, she picked up her papers and her briefcase and her low-grade opinions of nurses today, and left the hotel.

'No wonder,' Rose said. 'I don't know how she could work there. That's the room where the old man died. Sitting at his desk, Miss Mumford said, counting the money he'd never spent on other people.'

'Every old house has rooms people have died in,' her mother said. 'Dr Pomeroy left because her work was finished. I thought you loved the annexe, Rose, with what we've done there, and all the colours.'

'I do and I don't.' Rose shrugged. She had felt like shrugging all day, out of temper for some reason. She did like the annexe, but it still wasn't quite right. Nothing seemed right.

'She's been programmed against it by those silly Mumfords,' her father said.

'Or my silly self?' Rose invited him to quarrel, but he wouldn't.

She was a bit silly now, had been for weeks, restless, changeable, enjoying the increasing business at the hotel, with its promise of summer, then grumbling at the extra work. Wanting something without knowing what it was. Wanting another miracle? There were no such things. Feeling there was something she had to do. Not wanting to do anything.

Odd things irritated her for no reason. Hazel's thick legs, going round and round on her bicycle. Mrs Ardis, carrying things so slowly up the stairs, with a hand on her heart if

26

anyone was looking. This morning, poor old Moonlight stood on her toe and she swore at him, which she never wanted to do, because everyone else did. Even Mr Vingo, whom she liked, had usurped Rose's favourite turret room and driven a guest off the verandah, and the thought of Dr Pomeroy, moodily downgrading nursing student papers in the annexe lounge, still nagged at her.

'I bet she saw the ghost of the old man,' she nagged at her mother.

'Oh rubbish.'

'It could be haunted.'

'Double rubbish.'

'It's cold and damp.'

'Not any more, with this warmer weather. Even that wretched door stays shut now.'

'Damp makes doors stick, not open.'

'Well, the floor has settled, I expect.' Rose's mother was doing accounts at her desk, and only half listening.

'No one will want to stay there.' Her mother did not answer. 'Mollie! I said, no one will want to stay there.'

'Stop it, Rose.' Her mother looked up, and her father said, 'Don't call your mother Mollie,' and they were off into one of the quarrels she didn't want, but had to start.

You treat me like a child. . . . You behave like a child. . . . You don't let me do anything I want. . . . What do you want?

'What's wrong with you, Rose?'

'I don't know . . .'

'Just adolescence,' her father said drily, and Rose yelled, 'Oh – you don't understand!' and flung out of the room, stamped through the kitchen and out of the back door, running through the grass and out of the gate into the dark wood. On the damp path, where the tree trunks were smooth and calmly rooted, and the leaves carried on their business with the sky far above, she slowed and cooled down. She walked to the edge of the wood and out on to the sunlit moor, wandering about in an unfamiliar way. She never took walks by herself. She hiked across the moor to the castle ruins with the school campers, or went for bicycle rides with friends, or walked down to the village shops or the beach or the bus stop, always with a purpose. But now she pushed up through the bushes and over the wall and across the pasture to walk on towards the open moor in no particular direction, following a sheep track that skirted rocks and gorse bushes and ambled about, in the timeless way of sheep.

Rose felt better. The anger was gone. She began to feel like herself, and that same tune came into her head to keep time with her feet, that lilting tune that was both familiar and strange, with words that were not words, but sounds that beat out a rhythm like a horse on the turf, and then the descending notes, a long, powerful snort into the wind.

There were no riders in sight. No ponies on this part of the moor, no free horses grazing, but the air seemed full of the heady scent of a horse, and her heart quickened to the idea that she might see that marvellous grey horse again, the most beautiful horse in the world. As she walked on smiling, the path became unfamiliar. It straightened out, and there were no sheep droppings, or marks of the hard little hoofs in wet places. The hills ahead of her were the wrong shape. If she could see that pointed one with the streamer of cloud coming off the top, she ought to be nearly at the lake. Where was it? Where was she? Better turn back before she got lost, back to the hotel to be her old self and start doing some work. Lay tables, start the salad.

The path turned, and a huge rock like a very large man was ahead of her, dark grey, glistening on its shoulders as if it were raining. Beyond it was a thicket of untidy trees, growing close together so that it was hard to find the path through the undergrowth. She wanted to turn back, but she had to push on through the trees, and out of them into a sudden swirling mist.

28

She could not see anything in front of her, she could not see the path, could not even feel the path when she put a cautious foot forward. The tune came again into her head, and somewhere before her and below, as if the ground dropped away, a faint light began to glow and pulsate in the mist.

Marsh gas. She knew about that. A marsh was no place to be when you could not even see the ground under your feet. She turned and groped back to where the path led away over the rising and falling moorland, already in the distance showing its half tones of reds and mauves and grey-blues, as the sun went down. How strange to run into such a sudden dense pocket of mist. Curiosity made her turn back to the looming giant rock and walk round it again, and through the trees. There was no mist, no marsh, no drop in the ground, only the gravel at the edge of the small lake they called Noah's Bowl, with a few small sea birds that had come inland to sit on the quiet grey water.

CHAPTER FOUR

Mr Vingo spent most of the time in his room, but came down to the dining-room for meals.

'You looked flushed,' he told Rose, as she put his soup down on to the small table where he sat in the corner.

'I went for a walk.'

He had rather long and untidy black hair, which Mrs Ardis said he dyed, but Rose could see that the roots were just as dark at the parting. Being a waitress made you very familiar with the tops of people's heads.

'Where did you walk?'

'Up on the moor. I went to the lake.'

'You must have been running.' With his soup spoon raised, he looked up at her and lifted a curved black eyebrow.

'I was.'

Almost, she told him about the mysterious galloping grey horse, and how she had run back along the winding sheep track, away from the awesome rock and the sudden inexplicable mist that had blotted out Noah's Bowl, but she had all the other carrot soups to hand round from the hatch between the dining-room and pantry, where her mother was ladling out.

When she came back to the corner to take Mr Vingo's soup bowl and put down his shepherd's pie, he said, 'The lake on the moor? I must go there some time,' as if the conversation had not been interrupted.

'Everyone does. Hikers, riders, campers. Sometimes people come with spades and dig bits of it up because they want to find some more ruins of the castle that was there once – three or four hundred years ago, I think it was.'

'Three hundred, three thousand, three hours ago . . . time makes no difference.'

'Why?' Rose didn't care for people talking in riddles.

Mr Vingo wheezed, as he did when he did not want to say any more, and the large whites of his eyes bulged as if he was going to choke, but he picked up his fork and started to shovel in the potato part of the shepherd's pie.

Rose liked him all right, because he talked to her as if she was really there, which was more than some people did when you were waiting on them at meals, or bringing up their early morning tea.

She was not supposed to take tea up to the male guests, but Hilda thought Mr Vingo didn't count. If Rose knocked on the door of the turret room, he would call out, 'Greetings, Rose of all the world,' knowing it was her from her tread on the winding stair. Sometimes as she put the tray down outside the door, she could hear him huffing and puffing to get up, and crashing about in the bed that sloped towards the middle of the floor. Sometimes he would already be up and playing the piano. She would stand outside and listen, even if she was late for school, until he finished on a running chord and called out, 'How do you like that, Rose of all roses?' knowing she was still there.

If the sun was out, he might sit on the verandah with his stomach spreading above his trousers like a large egg in an egg cup, and he sometimes went out for a walk in the rain, which he liked. Later that week, Rose overtook him on her way back from the shops in the village. He was stumping along in his tight grey coat, with his blue rain hat turned up all round.

'Let me help you.' He turned down the brim of his hat to let the water out, then turned it up again and took one of her shopping bags.

'Thanks. I had to pick up some extra stuff. More people are coming for the weekend.'

'They must like crisps then.' Mr Vingo looked into the bag.

Rose giggled. 'Well – it's this family who come here. They have a young son Harry, and Ben who's a bit older than me.'

'I understand.'

But he couldn't, couldn't possibly understand how it felt to know that the Kellys were coming.

'Don't go too fast.' He panted beside her, with his hair straggling slickly down the sides of his face and his feet waddling outwards, and once again she almost confided in him, almost told him that she was on the hop because Ben was coming.

When the Kellys arrived, Rose dodged into the kitchen, because she did not want to greet them in the hall if Ben was not going to notice her. Emptying the dishwasher, she heard Mr Kelly's slow boom and Mrs Kelly's high rattling voice, and as they went up the stairs, with Harry whining, 'It's too heavy!' she heard Ben ask, 'Where's Rose?'

Her mother must have told him, because the swing door of the kitchen opened and he put in his head, nut-coloured curls cropped surprisingly short this year, and said, 'Hullo!' brightly to Rose and Hilda, but took his head out again before Rose could say anything.

But he did notice her this year. Incredibly, he dragged her out to walk on the sand dunes, and climbed the slopes of hollows and rolled down in the sand, as if he did not care about trying to be grown up.

When they stood on a tufted crest to watch the edge of the quiet sea endlessly creeping, retreating on the stony beach and he asked her, 'How's it going?', she wanted to tell him about the strange upheavals in her normally dull and pre-dictable life, but she shrugged and said, 'Oh – same old thing.'

'I heard you did something brave.'

'Me?'

'You put out a fire.'

'Who told you that?'

'Hilda.' Guests were not suppose to go into the kitchen, but Ben liked to go in and chat to Hilda or Jim or whoever was working back there. He could be funny and charming, and could get cake or an apple any time he wanted.

'Oh, that.' Rose scowled. 'It was only a tiny fire.' At the time it had seemed like a conflagration, but it couldn't have been. 'It was nothing.'

Nothing compared to the dramas Ben unfolded about his school, and being in the athletics team as a long distance runner, which was why he had cut his hair, for streamlining, and how this person had been sent down for drugs and that one for alcohol, and . . . He pulled up Rose's hand to look at her giant watch, which told the date as well as the time.

'Half past Easter! Gotta go. I'm late.'

With Ben, you didn't ask, 'What for?', and he didn't tell you. He ran away without waiting for her, bounding up and down over the shallow dunes like an antelope.

On Sunday afternoon, Ben's mother, who talked to everybody, whether they wanted it or not, persuaded Mr Vingo to play his piano for some of the guests.

'Going to the concert?'

After serving lunches and helping to clear, Rose had homework. Her father had roused her from a daydream, staring out of the sitting-room window down the long back garden and the wood.

'Are *you*?' she asked.

'Not I.' He prided himself of not being a joiner.

'Nor me. I've got to do this damn stuff.'

'You weren't working.'

'I was thinking.'

'Don't scowl. You'll fix those lines on your forehead. Go on. This might help your piano lessons.'

'Nothing could help them.'

But Ben, who was the only customer who ventured into their family rooms without being invited, put his head round the door and said, 'Come on, Rose,' so she went.

Half a dozen people were crowded into the turret room, its size already reduced by Mr Vingo and the little upright piano, which was made of some veined orange-coloured wood, and stood across one curve of the wall under a curving window. They sat on chairs and the bed and the carpet, which never stayed flat because of the slope. Rose sat on the floor by the door, in case she wanted to sneak out.

Mr Vingo sat with his back to them on the round piano stool, his buttocks overflowing it on each side, the ends of his hair hanging over the neck of his grey sweater, one side of his shirt collar out, one side in. He coughed a bit, cracked the knuckles of his thick fingers, then swirled the creaking stool round to face his audience shyly.

'What do you want me to play?' He looked as if he regretted it already. His big wet eyes were sad, and his broad pale face had a nervous twitch.

'Some golden oldies,' Mrs Frolich wanted. She and Mr Frolich went in for ballroom dancing contests in sequinned tulle and a cutaway coat.

'Ragtime.' Ben beat a rhythm on his knees.

'No, no, no.' Mrs Kelly jumped up from the bed and took over the audience. 'The whole point of this dear little gathering is that Mr Vingo is going to play us some of his *own* work.'

'Am I?'

'What you're working on now you promised come along now you know you did now don't say no there's a good man.' She ran her sentences together, so that you could not get a word in.

34

Mr Vingo raised his massive head and looked round the room seriously. 'I'm setting an old legend to music, you see. It's the story of a great happening hundreds of years ago, a heroic deed that saved a lot of poor and innocent people from the tyranny of evil and a ghastly death.'

'Oh it's too moving the Middle Ages I expect you mean we did them at school centuries ago evil and violence were rife you talk about dictators they had them then and God knows the common people needed a hero to save them.'

Mrs Kelly nodded to encourage him and sparkled her eyes. She was not really a silly woman, it was just that she had to talk.

Mr Vingo plodded on solemnly. 'The hero was a horse.' Rose looked at him. 'The music is called *The Ballad of the Great Grey Horse*. An immortal creature of grace and nobility, crusading against evil and sorrow by the force of his beauty and strength. His peaceable – peaceable –'

As he leaned foward to gasp, the stool tipped on the sloping floor, but he righted it and swung away from them to the piano and crashed out some mighty chords. Mrs Kelly opened her mouth to speak, Ben said, 'Mother . . .' warningly, and Mr Vingo began to play.

Rose was tired. She had got up early to ride. She had helped to serve thirteen lunches and lost the fight with the algebra. The music sent her off, leaning against the wall, with her head dropped and her short hair swinging forward. Then all of a sudden she was awake, because the tune from the moor was in her head, was in this room, was in Mr Vingo's fingers, as he played it very sweetly and lovingly on his little marmalade piano.

'I know that tune,' Rose said abruptly.

'Ssh!' From Mrs Kelly, of all people.

Mr Vingo finished the tune on its little run upwards, and then dropped it down to the low reverberating drum notes of the base.

'I know that tune,' Rose said again stubbornly.

'You couldn't,' Mr Vingo said without turning round. 'I only wrote it this morning.'

He started the tune again – la da *da* . . . da-dle *dee*,' leaping up like a flute.

Rose scrambled to her feet and went out of the room. As she ran down the turning stair, the door of the room opened above her, and her mother called, 'Rose – what's the matter?'

She ran on, along the corridor, down the back stairs, through the scullery and out of the back door, running, running into the wood where the scaly bark of the fir trees was like black crocodile hide, and the young oaks bent their branches like curving forearms beckoning – 'Come *on*!'

She jumped over roots and through puddles. At the edge of the wood she stopped, panting, and wiped the mud off her shoes on the grass. Then through the bushes and over the wall to cross the broad pasture. A small flock of sheep moved closer together and turned towards her, with a blank Miss Mumford stare. She made a face at them and went under the wire at the gap in the top wall and up the slope to the open country, running desperately.

As she ran, the music was still in her head, the flute-like notes of Mr Vingo's piano keeping time with her pounding feet. And all the time there was fear – why didn't she turn and go home? – the fear that all too soon the winding sheep track her feet so obediently followed would straighten out into the lonely unknown path of trodden grass, the far off hills would change shape, and over the next rise, the great rock would suddenly be there, shining with damp. Up a steep slope, she crawled on her hands and knees, and – oh! As her head went over the top, there it was before her.

She knew she had to go on. She knew that as she rounded the bulk of the rock and found the path through the trees, the ground would disappear beneath her, her feet would disappear as she groped her way downhill, with the mist enclosing her. Descending, she gradually walked out of the mist into brightness, and saw that she was halfway down the side of a narrow valley. A river ran at the bottom between banks of greener grass. On the other side, there was a large outcropping of flat rocks, jutting out from the valley wall like a platform. As she paused to gasp for breath, the great grey horse appeared, bounding on to the rock with a clatter of hoofs to stand there with one foot raised, head up, grey mane blowing. Because of the brightness of the sun, which shone low over the edge of the valley, his coat was luminous, like – like ice on fire, a sort of pearly grey, aglow. His tail was a silver froth, like swift-running water leaping out between two boulders.

Had he got loose from some marvellous stable she did not know existed? What was she supposed to do? Was he a wild horse that she must catch and possess and tame? Had he seen her? With his ears curved forward like scimitars, he stared down the valley past scattered farm villages and cottages towards the coast, where, far away, a huddle of white shacks she had never seen before was crouched together, and tiny boats lay on the sunlit sea.

With a swing of his graceful neck he turned his head and lowered it to look at Rose. He snorted gently, and she went on towards him.

At the bottom of the valley, there was a primitive sort of bridge over the river, great mossy stones supporting rough wooden planks without a handrail. Rose stepped out on to the bridge with her eyes fixed on the horse, so as not to look down. In the middle, one of the planks was loose and slippery, and there were rotten holes in it. She had to look down, and saw the water shouldering its way past the stone pillars, dragging their bright green moss out into the current like floating hair.

Rose stood still in midstream, but it would be as bad to go

back as to go forward, so she jumped over a gap in the plank, jumped down to the grass and scrambled up on the other side. Standing below him, she could see his great size, and his hide pulsing and glowing as he breathed in the sunlight. His hoofs on the rock above her were enormous, striped ivory white and slate below the delicate pasterns and strong dark grey legs. He lifted a front foot and pawed impatiently, scattering lichen from the rock.

She did not want to be below those hoofs, so she moved to the left and went up among a jumble of small rocks to try to approach him from the side. If she could get a hand on him, grasp his long mane, she could pull off her belt and put it round his neck, somehow lead him down and back across the valley. That was what she must be supposed to do. As she came level with him, small against his size, he turned to face her, which was a good thing, because she would not have wanted to approach those powerful quarters from behind.

The low sun was very strong, blazing on his shoulder as she reached out a hand to touch him. He snorted and stamped and tossed his elegant head, and she drew back in fear from his dapple coat which seemed both white hot and coal black, and from his large, deep grey eye, in which her dizzied senses seemed to see reflections of mountains, water, strange shapes of people moving . . .

She sank to her knees on the rock beside him. How dared she think of catching him, possessing him? She was possessed by him, humbled, afraid.

Crawling backwards, she somehow managed to slide off the rock and drop down to the stony slope. She stumbled down the side of the valley to the bridge. After she crossed, slipping off at the end of the planks and soaking wet to the knees, she looked up once, with the cold water swirling round her legs, and saw him still standing there, immobile, aloof, his neck up and arched, head tilted, one ear forward and one back, a classic grey statue, with the top layer of his mane lifting like feathers in the light wind from the sea.

As she neared home, her own world returned. The barbed wire caught her sweater, as always. The sheep did not even look up at her. The trees were just trees. She was exhausted, hardly able to think, dizzy and confused about what had happened to her on the familiar, friendly moor. Her friend Hazel always told her, 'You're mad!' if she produced a difficult new idea, because Hazel's mind moved slowly. Perhaps she was mad then. Perhaps she was losing her mind.

Her mother was behind the registration desk, working on bills. Most grown ups, when you have been somewhere you don't want to tell about, will greet you with, 'Where have you been?' One of the good things about Mollie was that she never asked, 'Where have you been?' until she saw that you wanted to tell her.

She said, 'Look at you, you're exhausted. You're doing too much. I'll be glad when school is over.'

'I'm OK.' Rose looked down at her feet. Her shoes were muddy and the bottoms of her jeans were wet. 'I'll help with suppers.'

'No, you won't. Go and have a bath, and I'll bring something up to your room. Before you go up, just run over to the annexe for me, like a love. I left the tape measure there.'

'Won't it do in the morning? I'll get it before school.'

'I need it tonight. Go on. The keys are on the hook by the back door.'

Rose did not want to go to the annexe house in the gathering twilight. Instead of going out of the back door and across the two gardens to the other kitchen, she went out into the road under the street lamp to go in by the front of the house next door.

It was a brick house, like Wood Briar, but covered with

ivy that was squared off round the windows like a neatly clipped dog, with a steep roof overhanging like a frown. On either side of the front path, the small garden did its best with pansies and marigolds, and a few motheaten rhododendrons that would have to be replaced when there was time. The window trim and the front door, which Rose had always hurried past when the old man lived there, were now painted yellow. 'Like an ice cream shop,' Philip Wood said.

Rose went through the gate in the brick wall and up the steps. After a moment's hesitation, because there *was* something funny about this house, no matter what anyone said, she opened the door and quickly turned on the light in the hall. All right, house. I dare you.

The hall was bright and welcoming. Her mother had put a bowl of flowers on the table, because any day now there could be a sudden surge of guests and they would have to put people here. The annexe was waiting for them, newly painted, new rugs on the polished boards, long flowered curtains at the French windows that looked out to the orchard where Rose could see the apple trees leaning about in the waning light.

She liked the house again. Her father was right. She had been programmed by the Mumfords. Rose opened the door into the front bedroom. There it was, fresh and orange and yellow. The chrysanthemums rioted over the bedspread and curtains. Thank God to be back from the moor, to familiar things. Everything about the annexe reminded her happily of last winter: she and her mother working so hard in here, and the day the plumbers and carpenters were finished, and the man who rebuilt the fireplace, and they had had a small party.

She took the tape measure back to her mother and told her, 'I'll do suppers.'

'You don't need to. There's only seven. Mrs. Maddox has

left already, taking her cat, thank God, and the Kellys have gone. They said to say goodbye.'

So there it was. The only person she might have wanted to tell about the discovery of the valley and the marvellous, terrifying grey horse was Ben. They could have laughed about her losing her mind, because she knew that he sometimes imagined things too. He had told her that when he was winning the cross country race last term, his strides got longer and longer and his feet barely touched the ground and he knew that he was going to run off the edge of the world.

CHAPTER FIVE

In the end, the only person she was able to tell was Mr Vingo.

All week it rained, but by Friday the weather cleared and the hotel filled up for the weekend. There were some people from the town, some who were on trips, and a friendly couple in their thirties called Jake and Julie, who often came for summer weekends from their jobs and their flat in a large strident city seventy miles away. Jake even plunged into the cold surf with the maniac swimmers who forced themselves into the sea all the year round. One of them was an old man of eighty who was expected to die of it every winter, but never did.

Dilys, one of the college students, came to be a waitress, her long hair pulled back into a thick plait down her back, which made her look not much older than Rose.

Brisk, bustling Gloria was 'on the rooms', with Mrs Ardis huffing along in her wake, threatening to quit, as she did every month in the summer because there was too much work, and every month in the winter, because it was boring.

Good old Hazel was coming from the village on Saturday afternoon to help in the kitchen and serving pantry, and stay for supper with Rose.

Saturday was the kind of day that Rose liked. Time to go out in the morning and run on the beach with Jake and Julie and their dog, which they kept in the kennel behind the hotel. Too busy all the rest of the day to open any of the books she had brought from school.

But all day she was like a shaken-up bottle of lemonade.

During the week, she had asked her mother, 'Are there any wild horses still on the moor?'

'I doubt it. Its become a tame sort of place now, with all the trekkers and trackers and diggers and joggers.'

'I saw one . . .' No. She realized at once that she couldn't say that. 'I dreamed I saw a beautiful grey one.'

'You dream of horses every night, don't you?' Her mother hugged her. She still had to bend a bit to do it, though Rose expected to grow taller and narrower soon. Getting your upward growth late meant your energy had gone into your brain, her father had explained to her when he was in an optimistic mood.

Out on the blustery beach with Jake and Julie, Rose kept thinking she saw the horse's crest and his plunging hoofs in the surge of the surf, where the big waves soared and crashed and tumbled in to be sucked back into the sea. She ran like a mad thing down the beach, with the brown dog barking and jumping round her, swerving in and out of the frothing sea, trying to see the flying mane as the waves crested and broke.

'What's got into you?' Jake and Julie laughed at her as she hurled herself back to where they were walking hand in hand.

'I've gone mad!' she shouted, and ran past them.

The pressure of suspense was still fizzing in her, choking up against the top of her throat. She could not run away from it.

After teas on the sunny verandah glassed in from the wind, Mr Vingo, who had sat like a buddha, smiling but silent with his teacup held on the mound of his stomach, got up, dusted off cake crumbs inefficiently and said to Rose, 'Come up to my room when you have a moment.'

Rose left the rest of the clearing to Dilys, who was in love and had been crying to Mollie in the scullery, and went upstairs in her blue and white check apron.

He was sitting in the armchair, which was too small for him. Once in, he had a hard time getting up and out.

'What did you want, Mr Vingo?'

She had learned from her mother that 'What do you want?' was crude. 'What did you want?' was all right.

'It's what *you* want, Rose of all the world. Want to talk?'

'What about?' She did not know if she could trust him. He had played her tune, but she had been half asleep after all. He could have been playing something else, and she had dreamed her tune.

He folded his hands across the cake crumbs and waited.

'That little tune,' she ventured. 'The one that goes up like a fountain, and then drops.'

He did not say anything, so she put it as a question. 'That little tune? You must have thought I was a dope running out of the room like that.'

'Not at all. You had somewhere to go?'

'Out to the moor.' She laughed without smiling. 'Don't ask me why, but I sort of had to. And then I saw . . . there's this valley, you see, I never knew it was there. I got lost. I couldn't find the lake, but there was this valley, running down to the coast, I'm not quite sure where, and there's a lot of mist from the sea. And it was –' she dug her toe at the carpet ('Don't dig at the carpet': her father) – 'it was there I saw the horse.'

'Tell me.'

'A shining grey.'

'Beauty and strength. Nobility without violence.'

'Is that what you said at the concert? I was only half listening. Listen . . . Mr Vingo, about that tune you played when I ran out.'

'Ah yes. That tune.'

'You said you just made it up, but I'd heard it in my head before.' She crossed her hands under her apron and held on to her stomach, as he was doing. 'I don't know, I mean – so am I psychic? Am I going mad or what?'

'You are thirteen, aren't you?'

44

'Sometimes I wish I wasn't. It's supposed to be the answer to everything. You know, the teens. End of childhood.'

'Just a beginning?' He smiled. Although his lips were thick and pale, they lifted at the corners into a very sweet, simple smile across the bottom of his broad face.

'Beginning of what?'

'Rose! Where are you?'

Rose opened the door and yelled down, 'I'm coming!' and turned back to him. 'Beginning of what? What's happening to me? What do you know?'

As he opened the smile to speak, Gloria yelled again, 'Rowze!'

'What?' She and Gloria were not supposed to yell at each other when there were guests in the hotel.

'Hazel's here!'

'You go down to your friend,' Mr Vingo said comfortably.

'She can wait. She's too early.' Hazel always timed things wrong.

'No, no, we'll talk again. There is plenty of time.'

Hazel was not Rose's best friend. She had no best friend now that Abigail had gone with her parents to America. There were several people she hung about with at school, two who rode at the same stable and one who had her own horse; but Hazel was the one she bicycled home with.

They were not only friends because they lived close. They had drifted together in the turbulence of school society, because they were both rather ordinary. In their class this year, there was a fashion for extremes and dramas. People went in for the heights and depths of neurosis, depression, allergies, dieting, wars against parents, genius, passion. Rose and Hazel simply plodded on down the middle of the road and tried to stay out of trouble.

Hazel was quite helpful at the hotel, fetching and

45

carrying between the kitchen and the serving pantry, and dishing out, her glasses steaming up as she bent over the soup. She was slow and deliberate, while Rose was fast and careless. She always said afterwards, 'I don't know how you can do this kind of stuff all the time,' whereas some people, like Abigail, envied Rose for being a hotel daughter.

Afterwards, they had their own supper in a corner of the dining-room, with pork crackling Mollie had saved when she was carving, and mountains of potato because Hilda had chosen to mash mountains today, and the remains of Mollie's famous trifle, which Rose had been worrying about when people started asking for seconds.

They were going to take Jake and Julie's dog for a walk, and scare themselves by creeping about among the low dunes in the dark, but it had begun to rain again.

'Better get on your bike before it gets worse.' Rose wanted Hazel to go home, so that she could continue talking to Mr. Vingo; but by the time Hazel had fiddled about and gone up and down stairs looking for her jacket, the rain was pelting down, so it was arranged that she would stay the night.

The bed in Rose's room was too small for both of them, and Hazel had been known to kick and swing out her fists in her sleep. There were no empty hotel rooms, so, as a treat, and if they would be angels and collect coffee cups and empty the ashtrays first, Rose's mother said they could sleep in the annexe.

'In the best bedroom?' Hazel had been taken into the front room to admire the chrysanthemums.

'You shall christen it.'

They took some fruit and biscuits over in case they got hungry in the night, and Hazel ate most of it before she even undressed. After very carefully folding the bedspread and putting it on the window seat, she sat on the edge of the wide bed eating, with the top of Rose's pyjamas tucked bunchily into the stretched elastic of the trousers. She wasn't exactly fat. Hazel wasn't exactly anything, neither clever nor stupid, pretty or ugly, gentle or violent. She was just solid.

'All solid muscle,' Rose's father described her, putting up an arm to ward off the thought of Hazel. 'She ought to be a lady wrestler.'

She looked nice and homey in Rose's pyjamas, with her glasses off and her hair freed from its rubber band and brushed out over her shoulders. Rose sat on the other side of the bed and asked without looking at her, 'Do you ever have that feeling, I mean – well, sort of – that there's something you've got to do?'

'I've done my homework.' Hazel was eating an apple.

'No, listen, Hay. Haven't you ever felt, I mean, sort of – well . . .' With her elbows on her knees, Rose put her hands into her short straight-cut hair and pushed it up above her ears, frowning. 'Sort of – this is going to sound weird – as if you were called to higher things?'

'Oh, shut up.' Hazel fidgeted on the bed and scratched her leg with a sandpaper sound.

Rose had told Hazel about the fire, though not about the bearded man on television, in case she had dreamed that, and Hazel had stared at Rose's hand and listened to the story of the miracle in the kitchen without saying anything. If you told her you had seen God, she would only stare, and absorb the information like a sponge.

'Do I look different to you?' Rose turned round. Hazel turned round too with the apple in her hand, and considered her for a bit before she said, 'No,' and looked at the apple to see where she would bite it next.

'Don't get apple on the blanket,' Rose said.

When they got into bed and turned out the light, Rose still wanted to talk, but Hazel went to sleep, snorting and thrashing about for a while, and then settling down like a dropped log, deep into the pillow.

47

Outside, the rain poured down. The street lamp showed streams of water on the window. Rose got up once to pull the curtains closer, and when she went back to bed she must have fallen asleep, because she woke suddenly from a dream she could not remember, and lay very still on her back, wondering what was different about the room.

She could still hear the rain. Hazel was still heavily asleep. Out of the darkness, furniture gradually appeared, the mirror on the dressing-table, the bedspread folded on the window seat, chairs with clothes on them. Rose had not wanted to put them in the cupboard, in case the door would not shut again.

It was not shut now.

Rose lay with her head turned stiffly, watching the door while she groped out a hand for the switch of the bedside lamp. She knocked the lamp and it fell on the floor. Probably broke the bulb. Hazel did not stir. After a long time of straining her eyes at the cupboard door and the darkness behind it, and holding herself small and still, Rose made herself swing her legs out of the bed and get to the light switch.

Even the bright overhead light did not wake Hazel. It showed the inside of the cupboard, harmlessly empty, and the door half open.

Because of the damp again. Rose put her mother's cheerful voice into her head.

She shut the door and it stayed shut. She tiptoed away round the end of the bed, turning back quickly to catch it at its tricks, but it gave her a blank yellow face.

She wished it wasn't raining. She wished Hazel had not had to stay the night, and that she was in her own room high up at the back of Wood Briar; but she climbed into the wide bed which was as comfortable as a nest, and went back to sleep.

She woke again in fear. The cupboard door was still shut,

but her dream had been awful, one of those dreams where you can remember the mood, but not the details, and the mood was sorrow, and it was still with her.

She tried to wake Hazel.

'What's the matter?'

'Let's go back to the hotel and sleep in the lounge.'

'Oh, shut up.' Hazel kicked her legs about and was asleep again.

The night was endless. Rose did not know how much she slept, nor what was dreams and what was her own fear. Once, she thought the door was open again, and there was a hint of that damp sea smell in the room, but when she turned on the light, the door was shut. Once she woke to find that she was very cold. She groped towards Hazel for the bedclothes, and found that the blanket was still covering both of them. Once as she was struggling up out of another heavy dream of sadness, she heard someone weeping. Who? Who was weeping in the house? She came fully awake with her hair wet on the pillow. It was she herself who was crying.

The dream was gone, but she could not stop desperately sobbing. Hazel half woke and grunted, 'Shut up,' and went back to sleep, and when Rose took a shuddering breath and gave a last gasping sob, Hazel hit out at her in her sleep.

Would this night never end? Rose got up, turned on the light to make sure the cupboard door was still shut, and went to the window to look for the promise of dawn. The wind had risen. When she pulled back the curtain, silvery flashes of rain were blowing sideways across the light of the street lamp. *The white flash of the dead man's spirit*, Miss Mumford had said, and for an instant, Rose thought she saw it, sweeping away with the rain.

She dropped the curtain, and crept back to the bed like a mole and burrowed under the sheets.

'You've talked half the night, I might have known it.'

When her mother pulled the curtains back and woke her out of her first good sleep, Rose could not believe that it was light and the rain had stopped and the night was over. The yellow cupboard door was shut. Hazel was in the bathroom, running water. The room was its old bright self. She turned on her back and smiled up at Mollie, in a bright blue sweater and the first airing of her white summer skirt.

'Rose, you look a wreck.'

Rose put a finger under her eye. No tears there, but her head ached. 'I cried in the night,' she said.

'Why, darling?'

'I was sad.'

'What about?'

Rose shook her head on the pillow. 'It was all so dreadfully sad.'

'I know those dreams.' Her mother bent to stroke her hair. 'They seem to come out of some depths of our primeval past, don't they, with the sadness of all the centuries.'

As soon as possible after the breakfasts were done and Hazel had bicycled away into the beginnings of a sunny day, with the rain steaming up off the road, Rose went to look for R. V. Vingo.

He was in the rocking chair on the triangular verandah under his room, which still held a sliver of the early morning sun. He was wearing an outfit Rose had not seen before, a tweed suit too heavy for the day, with a leather-buttoned waistcoat and a length of watch chain circumnavigating it.

'I've got to talk to you.' Rose stepped round the corner from the front verandah and shut the door.

'What's the matter?'

'Things are happening. Hazel and I slept in the annexe. They say I imagine things, and I know there's nothing wrong with the house really, but there is.'

His black eyebrows went up and he nodded and kept his

50

chin down on his crooked bow tie, looking up at her under the eyebrows.

'There's a door there that wants to open all the time. There were weird dreams. I woke up feeling cold when it wasn't cold. Once I woke up and someone was crying, and it was me. Why? Has this got anything to do with that tune, and the grey horse I saw? Mr Vingo, you seem to know something. You must tell me.'

'Yes, I must tell you.' He lifted his head and sighed. 'I thought we had time. But we haven't. It's beginning to happen now for you.'

'What is?'

'Sit down.'

She sat opposite him on the wicker stool. Over her shoulder, she glimpsed someone behind the glass top of the door, who looked at them, but went away.

'The music I am writing,' he began, and his fingers played the piano on his knees.

'You said it was about an old legend.'

'Strictly speaking, it's history. Legends aren't necessarily true. This one is, but it's been long forgotten, and it can't be told properly in words. Only in music, to be understood by those who are worthy to know.'

She wanted to ask, 'Like me?', because she had heard the tune, but did not want to sound conceited.

'Hundreds of years ago – oh, almost four hundred years, let's say, it doesn't really matter – the people with money and position and power didn't care much about all the others. In fact, they had no idea how the poorer people had to live. There were –' He took a deep breath – 'Well, there were nobles and dukes and things, and they gave money and soldiers to the king and got a lot of land and privileges in return. There were merchants, who made money off everybody, and there were the small farmers and insignificant peasants, who were totally dependent on the good will of the local high muck-a-muck to be able to survive. You've done history. You know all that.'

'Sort of. What's it got to do with –'

'Peace.' Mr Vingo held up a hand, plump pink palm outward. 'Let's get local. You know about the old castle on the moor?'

'The old ruins? There's only a few stones left.'

'Fallen to ruin, as all evil edifices must do in the end. The man who lived there called himself the Lord of the Moor, though he had no right to the title. He was a cruel little weasel of a man, who kept a bloodthirsty weasel as a pet. He not only robbed the poor people of their common grazing land, but forced them to pay him for the doubtful privilege of living below his castle on the hill.'

'How could they, if they were so poor?'

'Cows, sheep, grain. The favourite daughters to slave in the castle as servants and marry his crude, rotten soldiers.'

For the first time, Mr Vingo was talking fast and easily, not wheezing and stammering as he usually did.

'One beautiful daughter had a son, who . . . Enough of that, we haven't got much time. This you must know, Rose. When that boy was about your age –' he nodded at her solemnly – 'the Lord over-reached himself in beastliness and all the people would have been killed, but they were saved by the bravery of the boy and of the grey horse who was the favourite charger of the Lord of the Moor.'

'The Great Grey Horse,' Rose said. 'I heard you say that at the concert before I fell asleep.'

'And the people idolized him as the noblest of all living creatures: courage and beauty and peaceable strength.'

'A thirteen-year-old *boy*?'

Mr Vingo shook his head.

'The *horse*?'

'What else?' He leaned forward over his tweed paunch,

with his large prominent eyes fixed on Rose, crouched on the low stool at his feet.

'His mission is to protect innocent people from evil and misery and violence.'

'How?'

'Can't tell you now.' Mr Vingo's eyes were watering. He was running out of breath. 'You'll know later. Just know about . . .' he paused. 'The Great Grey Horse.'

'I saw him,' Rose whispered.

Mr Vingo nodded and began to breathe heavily.

'You played the tune, and I had to go there. You knew. Why didn't you tell me before?'

'Timing, timing, Rose. Timing is everything. I had to wait till you were ready. So did he. Now – now, when your life is travelling through that – that special age –' He was losing breath – 'When your mind and spirit are aroused to a state of tempestuous movement . . .'

'You mean, being thirteen?'

'Understand that you are one of the chosen, who can reach him, and respond and – and – and obey.'

Mr Vingo began to cough. Water streamed from his eyes. He pulled out a handkerchief and put it over his face, rocking backwards in the wicker chair, and plummeting down with his feet flat on the floor boards.

The spell was broken. Rose shook herself. 'You made it up. People don't obey horses. Horses obey people.'

Mr Vingo came up out of the handkerchief. 'Not this one.'

'You're trying to frighten me. I wish I hadn't told you about the annexe. You're trying to make me more scared.' Out of the corner of her eye she was aware of someone's shadow beyond the glass door, watching them again. 'I don't believe it.'

'I'm sorry, Rose.' Mr Vingo's great chest went up and down, and he smiled sadly at her. 'You have no choice.'

She left him abruptly.

Later that day, he was gone. He had disappeared completely, leaving behind the piano and most of his clothes.

'Did he pay his bill?' Philip asked Mollie.

'Not yet, but he will when he comes back.'

'He'd better,' Philip said grimly. 'What were you talking to him about this afternoon, Rose?'

'I don't know . . . Things.'

'I'm not sure I trust that character. For two pins, I'd get a van down and have the damn piano and all his stuff carted away.'

'Oh, Phil,' Mollie said soothingly.

'I mean it. I don't want you getting too friendly with him, Rose.'

'I like him.' She was not going to say, 'He frightened me.'

'I don't like either of you being too chummy with any of the customers. I've told you that.'

'But that's part of the charm of Wood Briar,' Mollie said.

'It's not professional.'

'Yes, dear,' Mollie said, and Rose said, "Yes, Daddy.' They had heard this before.

CHAPTER SIX

Nothing changed. That was the deceptive thing. One day Rose's life was in a turmoil, and the next, everything was back to normal.

Her mother and father were the same as always. Her mother working like a demon, with damp tendrils of hair on her flushed cheeks, hurtling in and out of crisis when the fishmonger didn't deliver or the plumbing got stopped up, but always smiling for the guests. Her father returning from work sometimes early, sometimes late, sometimes cheerful and wanting to swim or take the little boat out, sometimes bitter about his job and his boss at the laboratory who was stupider than he.

School was the same, limping towards the end of term as if it would never get there. Rose was the same. She rode in the late afternoon now that it was lighter, out on to the moor with a string of riders, and Moonlight put his foot in a rabbit hole that everyone else avoided. The moor was the same.

They rode past the flat-topped hill on the other side of the lake, and Rose asked Joyce if she knew any legends about the old ruins up there.

'Did hear something once. Shorten your reins, Rose, and don't let that beggar snatch at trees. Bunch of rubbish though.'

'What did you hear?' Rose kicked Moonlight to catch up with Joyce's long-legged, striding horse.

'Can't remember. Fairies and goblins or some such rot. All *right*, everybody! Stop loafing about and let's see if we can get these nags into a ter-*rot*!'

The moor was the same. With Mr Vingo gone, it was easier to try to put off thinking about what he had told her. Everything was the same.

Some of the same people were turning up at the hotel. Spring visitors who liked to come before the summer tourists. Fishermen who went out in Jim Fisher's brother's boat, and got Mollie to fry their fish for them. Rose was as glad to see people come back as Mollie was. It tied your life to the safe cycle of the year, like knowing that the birds would come and go, and that even as the leaves fell off the trees in autumn, they were being pushed by the embryo growth of next year's buds.

One of the welcome events was Martin and Leonora turning up in their van for lunch, as they did every spring when he had to go to the hospital for a check-up. Rose helped Leonora and Jim to tug the wheelchair up the shallow front steps. Martin was strong and healthy from the waist up, but his legs had been paralysed after a crushing steeplechase fall two years ago. Rose was fascinated by him, because he seemed as relaxed and happy as if nothing were wrong, and was more interested in other people than in himself. She wanted to talk to him about horses, but perhaps this was a forbidden subject now.

Leonora, who had given up a ballet career to look after him, was the kind of woman Rose would love to grow up to be: slender and graceful, with long straight black hair and gentle, shining eyes in a lovely pale face. Some hope. Several new people were arriving too. A family of four and a half (one was a baby) were staying for a month until their new house was ready. The car people began to turn up every evening demanding rooms without reservations and taking off next morning without even seeing the sea, leaving beds, beds, beds to change for Gloria and Mrs Ardis and a flighty young girl called Cindy from the drug

56

treatment centre, who told Rose that going to gaol couldn't have been worse than cleaning bathrooms.

They were using the annexe now, and everyone loved it. When Jake and Julie came the next weekend, Mollie offered them the best front bedroom as a favour.

Rose did not see much of them. They did not seek her out. After lunch, Jake went off somewhere in the car, and she saw Julie crossing the road towards the dunes alone, with the dog. She could not find them after dinner when she looked for them to play Scrabble, so she took care of the baby while the family of four – husband and wife, grandmother and divorced daughter – went to the cinema. That night, from the baby's room at the back of the hotel, a full moon night, a night for dogs to howl for no reason, Rose heard Jake and Julie's dog whining and barking from the kennel.

Julie did not come to the dining-room for the big Sunday breakfast – choice of kippers or sausage and bacon and egg, or both. Jake usually had both. This morning, he just wanted toast. Gloria was waiting on him, but he stopped Rose as she went by his table.

'I know you don't do room service,' he said, 'but could you possibly take something over to Julie when you've got a moment – coffee and toast?'

'You can make that for her in the annexe kitchen,' Rose said.

'I offered.' Jake's long thin face was mournful. 'She wouldn't let me get her anything. But if you just take a tray over . . .'

Rose knocked at the bedroom door and went in. Julie was in bed in a dim light, so she put down the tray and pulled back the curtains.

'Look – it's a lovely day. Don't you feel well?'

'I'm all right,' Julie said, not looking up. She pushed herself up against the pillows and tried to smile. 'Thanks, Rose, but I don't want anything.'

'You must have breakfast.' Rose put the tray on her lap. She had picked a rose from the garden as she came through and put it in a glass, but Julie didn't notice.

'Jake's worried about you.'

'I doubt it.' Julie set her mouth.

'Julie!' If this marriage went wrong, nothing was secure.

'This has been a horrid weekend, for some reason. Jake's moody. I'm in a bad temper. Yesterday, he took that – that girl – the one with the baby – off to the art museum because she'd never been before.'

'But you've been there.'

'Yes,' Julie said, meaning, 'You don't understand.' She picked up the cup and began to weep into the coffee, trying to sob and drink coffee at the same time.

Later that day, Rose went over to the annexe to collect towels, and heard Julie weeping again. But their red car was not in the hotel car park, and her mother told her that they had left.

It was only a matter of time. Mr Vingo did not return, but the haunting little tune drifted through her head at odd times, and she knew she could not avoid the horse for ever.

Once, she heard the ascending flute notes of the tune through the roar and rush of the dishwasher in the scullery. Once, the low, reverberating notes, like a horse snorting into the wind, were revolving in the engine of her father's noisy old car. When she and Hazel went to an afternoon pop concert on Newcome Pier, Rose heard the melody again, weaving its way through the jagged rock music of a local group in pirate hats and pink running shorts.

'I've got to go,' she shouted urgently at Hazel, through the noise. Hazel picked up Rose's wrist to peer at her watch. 'It's not half over.' Her words were blotted out in a crash of electronic sound, but her lips were obviously protesting, 'We've paid.'

'You stay. I'm off.'

Hazel shrugged, and continued to move her large knee solemnly up and down, slightly off beat. Rose clambered over her, pushed her way past several elderly holiday-makers who were being deafened by the music if they weren't deaf already, and ran back down the pier to get her bicycle. She rode through back streets, and full tilt out towards the moor.

She came on to it up the road that led to the stables, turning along the edge of the wood and hurling the bicycle in the bushes, to run up to the wall and across the pasture, not thinking, not afraid, drawn forward by some force far stronger than herself.

This time, as she rounded the rock with her heart pounding, and groped her way down through the mist, she became aware that somewhere around her in the valley, shadowy, undefined figures were moving. The blood that drummed in her head had become the murmur of rough voices. She heard an oath, a sound like the rattle of chains, in front of her a man's laugh, so close that she stopped and turned to go back, but there was someone else behind her. She couldn't see him, but there was an acrid smell of sweat, and she could hear his breathing.

The horse . . . She had got to keep going, and break out into the sunlight to reach the horse. She took one or two timid steps down, with her hands out to feel her way, when a patch of mist drifted away, and for a clear moment before the vapour closed in, she saw a huge figure in a cloak right in front of her. His face was masked from nose to chin, and his eyes were slits of steel.

Rose stumbled sideways, and as she plunged on down beyond him, a hand brushed her shirt, and she heard the laugh again. Suddenly she was out of the mist and running down the last slope to the river, and the horse plunged out on to the rock with a great surge and clatter, his pearly coat a blaze of silver light.

His eyes were slits of steel . . .

'I'm coming!' she called. He tossed his beautiful head, and she thought, 'If I go to him, I'll never get back. I can't go back through that dreadful mist.'

On the bridge, she stopped and turned with a hand on the rickety rail, to risk a look behind her. There was no mist. No cloaked shapes, no threatening murmur of voices, no clink of steel or creak of leather. Only the slope of the valley, studded with rocks and bushes, a lark singing high in the sky at the top.

She crossed the bridge and climbed up the other side, her eyes fixed ardently on the shining horse who stood waiting on the rock above her.

She climbed round over the jumbled stones and stepped out on to a rock just above him on the other side, with a steep drop on one side, a rock wall at her back, and the great horse confronting her. As he turned his head, she saw herself, small and afraid, a tiny creature in the deep, wise grey eyes, and before she knew it, she was on his back. His bright, glowing skin did not burn. It was at the same time warm and cool, his back unbelievably soft, yet firm and safe. He rose, and with his long grey mane blowing like a pennant in her face, they were away – galloping, flying – she could ride!

On Moonlight, there were always two moving parts, her and the five-legged horse, and they never meshed to move in unison. With this horse she was part of him, and he of her. It went on for ever. The wind roared by, and the sensation of speed and rhythmic power put her into a kind of trance, through which she became aware of a voice, echoing far away at first, then closer and sharper.

'Felicity! Fe-li-ci-tee! Help me! Help – Police!'

Her hand was on the latch of a small iron gate, a latch that felt familiar to her thumb as she pushed it down and opened the front gate of the annexe house. *Was* it the annexe house? The front garden was nothing but rank grass and overgrown bushes. The tangled ivy was pulling away from the walls and straggling across the window where the old woman poked out her grey, disordered head and shouted, 'Help! He's killing me!'

'She's at it again.' A stout woman came through the gate behind Rose in a square fur coat and round fur hat, and shouted up at the window, 'Take it easy, Mum – it's only Joan and Felicity!'

The old woman shrieked like a seagull and disappeared suddenly from the window, as if someone had pulled her.

The stout woman was Rose's mother. She knew that. Just as she knew that she was not Rose, but Felicity, with long silky hair that hung in front of her leather jacket, and the kind of tight black trousers and shiny pointed boots that Rose would never wear. Curious. She was Rose and Felicity at the same time. Felicity was walking and talking. Rose was observing.

The upper window banged shut. 'Nothing changes,' Felicity's mother sighed. 'Oh well. Better get in and get it over with.'

Felicity walked up the weed-choked path to the peeling brown front door, but it was Rose who observed with surprise that the big blue and white sign – 'Wood Briar Hotel' – was gone from next door, and the old black and gold sign – 'The Cavendish' – was back, slightly lopsided, along the front edge of the verandah roof.

After a long time, the door was opened by a thickset old man with humped shoulders, his lower lip pushed up above the top one to reach his broad nose in a sniff.

'Hullo, Dad,' his daughter Joan said, falsely bright.

He grunted, and Felicity said, 'Hullo, Grandpa,' with natural cheerfulness, because for some reason she quite liked the old man and felt sorry for him.

He did not answer this either, but turned and shuffled, with his brown cardigan humped up short at the back, through the hall to a dark panelled room with a sulking fire in the small grate.

He sat down in a sunken leather armchair. Joan sat down without taking off her coat or her pale fur hat, and rubbed her hands. She had short thick brindle curls like a poodle, over a face that was broad like the old man's, but flushed with crimson veins from the cold, while his was pale and grey, as if he lived under a stone.

'Well, here we are,' she said, still trying to jolly him along.

'And about time too,' he grumbled.

'That's what you always say when we *do* come. No wonder . . .' She bit her lip. 'Never mind.'

'Where's your brother Mark?'

'You know he's in Venezuela. Really Dad.' She bit her lip and tried again. 'How's Mum?'

'Mad as a hatter.' He chuckled in a grisly way. 'You'll see. I forbade her to come down.'

'Shall we go up to her?'

'Nah,' he said in a sneering way. 'She'll come down, worse luck.'

Felicity knelt on the worn carpet in front of the fire, carefully, because of the crease in her trousers, and poked at the sluggish fire. It needed wood to rekindle it, and more coal, so she took the empty scuttle and went out through the kitchen to the coal shed.

The kitchen was dark, with dark wood cabinets and the terrible marbled linoleum, like the cover of an exercise book, that Rose remembered the decorators tearing up to put down the bright mosaic tiles. Outside, the bare grey apple trees had broken branches, and long coarse grass and weeds struggling up their trunks like fetters. A tree had blown down and lay on the grass, with an upper branch poking a ragged hole in the coal shed.

The door of the shed had lost a hinge. Beyond the small

63

pile of coal, the accumulation of years of tools and broken mowers and old crusted paint pots were cluttered up and draped with cobwebs.

Coming out with the coal, Rose saw the back of the hotel next door. Through a broken slat of the fence, she could see a prim garden with gravel paths leading nowhere, and signs that said, 'GUESTS ARE REQUESTED NOT TO . . . etc.' A cross-looking waiter in a black tail coat and bow tie came out of the back door and lit a cigarette. On the doors and windows was the ugly yellow-green paintwork that Rose's father had said looked like vomit when they bought The Cavendish four years ago.

Was it more than four years ago now? Was that it? Had she gone back in time? Rose was puzzled, but not afraid, that was the most puzzling thing about it. She felt quite at home being Felicity, neat and slim in her pointed boots, carrying the coal into the depressing kitchen with its sink and wooden draining board full of dirty china and saucepans. Yet she was still Rose, noting from a grease-smeared calendar stuck to the wall with a safety pin, that yes, it was five years ago.

Because she was Felicity, she knew that her grandfather had once been a successful political cartoonist, until he dropped out of style and had to take jobs he hated to support his family. He had grown more bitter, and now seemed to have holed himself up in his study at the back of the house, with the dusty curtains drawn across the French windows because his eyes could not stand the light. Bits of his clothing, outer and underwear, were strewn about. The desk was cluttered with papers and books and medicine bottles and filthy ashtrays and cups half full of cold tea. Piles of newspapers were on all the chairs. There was nowhere for Felicity to sit, so she sat on the floor by the resuscitated fire, which her grandfather complained was baking him.

He went through a string of complaints and criticisms against the house, the hotel next door, the government, the weather, and various members of his family, with particular reference to Joan's husband. Her face got redder as she got more annoyed. His only pleasure seemed to be to goad her. But when Felicity said, 'Come off it, Grandpa. Just because Daddy beat you at golf twenty years ago – ,' her mother snapped at her, 'Don't laugh at him!' and they all sat and scowled at each other.

Felicity fidgeted and sulked and flipped her long hair back and forth and finally got up with an impatient snort and went into the kitchen to put the kettle on for tea. She made some toast, and burned it under the awkward grill of the old gas stove. While she was scraping it at the sink, she suddenly felt very sad and hopeless. Holding on to the edge of the sink, in the same spot where Rose had wept over the broken yellow cups, she had to keep her eyes stretched wide open so as not to let tears wash away her eye make-up.

I'm so stupid. But she shook back her head and flipped her hair behind her shoulders and then smoothed it forward again in her habitual preening gesture, and went back to the study.

'Shall I bring the tray in here?'

'No, no, no.' The old man's chin went up and down. 'I don't want crockery all over my books,' although there were smeared glasses and dirty cups with teaspoons in them on every flat surface, which is why Felicity had not been able to find any spoons in the kitchen.

She picked up the tin tray with its scarred picture of an ancient regiment in India, which she remembered since she was tiny, and carried it across the hall to the dining-room. As she kicked open the door, she almost dropped everything.

Her grandmother was sitting at the table wearing a green satin dress with ruffles, and a large pink artificial flower pinned into the nest of her hair.

'Give you a surprise, eh dear?' she said quite normally.

Felicity put down the regimental tray and bent to kiss the air an inch away from the patchily powdered face, which had scarlet lipstick on one side of the mouth only. The other side was mauve, and the knotted hands were blue with cold. The old lady smelt of stale scent and vinegar and damp underwear.

'Waiting for my tea like a good girl, eh?' She smiled childishly up at Felicity and then winced the smile into fear and drew back, as the old man shambled into the room and asked her, 'What the hell are you rigged out like that for? You look like a clown at a funeral.'

'Why shouldn't I get dressed up when my dear ones come? Hullo, Joan dear. How you've grown.'

'At fifty, Mum, I've stopped growing,' Joan said, 'unless you mean sideways.'

The old lady behaved quite well, chattering in what sounded a normal way, except that the words did not make sense. When her husband said, 'Shut up,' and threw the only teaspoon at her, she shut up, and began to eat stale biscuits very fast, licking her long blue fingers to pick up the crumbs. Her fingers were so thin that a ring with a heavy carved green stone swivelled loosely.

Felicity, who was on a diet, ate only half a piece of toast, which was disappointing to Rose. Her mother began to tap her foot, always a bad sign. The grandfather swilled tea noisily.

'I suppose you'll all be mobbing in here for Christmas,' he said ungraciously.

'Not this year, Dad.' Joan had a way of shouting at him, although he was not deaf.

'You always come at Christmas.'

'That's why we're not coming this year.'

The old man pushed up his lip. The old woman looked anxiously back and forth between him and Joan, the pink flower wobbling.

66

'I'll come,' Felicity said impulsively. 'I like the beach in winter.'

'I have other plans,' her mother said warningly.

'I'll come on my own.'

'You know you don't want to.' Joan reddened under the fur hat, which had ridden up high on her thick springy hair, like a cheese soufflé. 'You're just trying to curry favour.'

'I'm not!' Felicity shouted and jumped up.

The grandmother shrieked, and her chair tipped backwards against the wall, and her hands flew up, sending her cup flying with them.

'Shut up, damn you!' The grandfather cursed at her, as she went on shrieking, and the shrieks filled Rose's head, dizzying her. She put her hands over her silken hair to cover her ears, and shut her eyes against her mother's disgust and her grandfather's anger, and the mad old woman's fearful face with the eyes rolled back, and spun dizzily away, away . . .

Rose opened her eyes to find herself lying on the ground with her hands over her short hair, a few yards away from the edge of the lake where the valley ought to be.

CHAPTER SEVEN

'You're back early,' her father said. When she put the bike away, he was at the other end of the shed, which he had rigged up as a summer work room.

'I thought I was terribly late.' Rose had run for home in a sort of daze, her legs navigating the moor by themselves, and had almost ridden all the nuts and bolts off her bicycle, jolting it headlong through the wood.

'Concert no good?'

'It was smashing.' She had to say that, because he had prophesied that it would be a third-rate group of degenerate local yobbos, splitting the air like chain saws.

'So you left early. Fifty-three, fifty-four, fifty-five.' He was counting coloured wine gums out of a large jar.

'I didn't,' she lied. On the way home, she had planned to explain her lateness by saying that the concert was long and she and Hazel had stopped to get something to eat.

'It must have been mercifully short.'

Rose looked at her watch. She had been at least three hours at her grandfather's house – Felicity's grandfather's house. Her watch showed that it was only about an hour since she had left Hazel at the concert.

'Dad.' He knew all the answers. Perhaps he could explain this.

'Sixty-two, sixty-four . . .'

Rose hung about in the work room, looking at the scales and the lighted magnifying glass and the photographs of past triumphs, like a doughnut-shaped pillow, and a rocking-horse, and a chocolate bar, which his research had proved to be bad for you.

'Dad.'

'Eighty-five, eighty-six – got em!'

'Got who?'

'Total weight of contents: 440 grams. Weight of single piece: 4.54 grams. Calculate for me, Rose. How many wine gums should be in the jar to make the weight claimed on the label?'

'Why not weigh them all together?' Rose's mind was far away from mathematics.

'Because the weight of the mass differs, according to distribution and the space between each, from the multiplied weight of a single piece. What was it you wanted?'

'It doesn't matter.'

'But you had your fists clenched.' He sometimes noticed more than you thought.

She unclenched them and went into the hotel. Up in her room, she changed her jeans for her waitress skirt, and stood in front of the mirror to see if she looked anything like Felicity. How did she know what Felicity looked like? She didn't, only what she felt like. Rose's hair, which needed cutting, was at odds and ends, with a few bits of dead grass in it from the moor. She picked them out, then made Felicity's flipping movements. Perhaps she would let her hair grow long. But then she would have to tie it back in the kitchen and the dining-room. Felicity would never have been allowed to flip her hair about over the food in this hotel.

Rose sighed, and tied her check apron round her waist, and went slowly down to help make sandwiches for tea (tea-time was long over at the old man's house), pondering as she trod on each step, trying to puzzle it out, as her father would if she gave the whole thing to him as a mathematical problem.

By the next day, she had already forgotten some of it, which did not seem to be right. Obey the horse, Mr Vingo had said. So she had gone to the valley and braved her way through those dreadful shapes and voices in the mist – or had she imagined them because she was afraid? She had flown with the horse where he wanted, and, in some dreamlike way, he had travelled her five years back through time and deposited her in the house next door, among those – those awful people. They weren't really awful though, as individuals. They were just awful together.

The old man was dead now. So was the old woman – he drove her to it, the Miss Mumfords had said – her eyes permanently rolled back in her head, as Rose had last seen her. What had they got to do with Rose, or she with them? Was the old man haunting the annexe now, because Mollie had made his dingy study into a bright comfortable little lounge? Or was it the old woman, because he had made her so unhappy there? Was there something Rose had forgotten? If she could just remember more about it, she might understand.

When the customers were out of the annexe rooms, she went across to help Gloria make the beds.

'Yoo-hoo!' Gloria called down from upstairs, as she heard Rose come in at the kitchen door.

Rose yoo-hooed back, but did not go up at once. These yellow cupboard doors, where the paint had not come out bright enough, had been dark wood. The calendar was up here. She felt for the hole made by the safety pin, but it was painted over. This shining sink had replaced the old stone one that Felicity had hung on to and tried not to cry. The same place where Rose had cried when she broke the cups, back then in the spring before she was thirteen, when life already seemed difficult and complicated. But those were the good old easy days, compared to now.

She went through to the hall. The door to the front bedroom was the door Felicity had kicked open, carrying the tin tray. The old woman had been so cold in there. Cold . . . so was Rose, when she slept there with Hazel.

Here was where the old man's study had been. This wide brick fireplace had been his cramped old iron grate. Beyond the open glass doors, she saw the flat stump of the tree that had fallen against his toolshed, rising above the mown grass.

'Rowze!'

'*Coming!*'

Where was the horse? Was he only in her head, as Rose had been inside Felicity's silken head, looking down at the sophisticated boots? What colour were those tight trousers? Rose was forgetting. She must go back there. She must find the horse again. She walked out across the moor, following a track to the right, towards Noah's Bowl, but she could not find the dark wet rock, or the valley. Had it all been just a single weird experience that would fade as she got older, and be mistaken for a dream? Would she never hear that tune any more, never again take that flying ride with the horse? She could not quite remember now how it had happened, how she had got on his back, how he had galloped through the air; only its intense and thrilling joy.

She even went up the crooked stairs to Mr Vingo's empty room, to try to pick out the tune on his piano. The door was locked on the outside, to foil any burglar who got in through the window. Mrs Ardis had made the bed up clean and tidied some of his things into piles of her own choosing. Books and a biscuit tin and his domino set and a hairbrush and a bottle of blackcurrant syrup. Shoes and a sweater and crumpled music pages scribbled over and crossed out, and a map and a pair of socks and a cheap white tin horse in mediaeval trappings, part of a set of toy knights, without his knight.

The marmalade piano was shut. Tilting slightly on the uneven floor, it looked like a horse resting one back leg while it waited to be used again. Rose approached it carefully and opened the lid. Softly, she tried to find the tune with one finger. Da da *dee* – going up like that – no, that wasn't right. She tried various combinations of black and white notes, but she could not recapture the tune.

School was over. Ben came back to Wood Briar with his family, and started to teach Rose how to run. He was in training for the 5,000 metre county championships, and Rose was to pace him, running along the beach with him in the early morning, with the low sun pushing their gawky shadows along the sand before them. She could not keep up with him if he ran fast, but he taught her how to breathe and to place her feet and move her arms, and she could stay beside him as far as the stone breakwater.

While she rested, he taught her the warming-up exercises he did before a serious run, and some of the resuscitation techniques he had been learning at school, 'in case we're on a long distance run and some silly beggar passes out.' He showed her how to breathe air into an unconscious person's lungs, how to feel for a pulse in the carotid artery, and if there was none, how to press on the breast bone with both hands to make the heart pump the blood through the air in the lungs and out to the brain before it died from lack of oxygen.

They practised the pressure on a round-bellied mound of sand, the same shape as Mr Vingo: pause to give two mouthfuls of air, fifteen presses. 'You keep on doing it until help comes. You keep on and on. You never give up.'

When they had saved the life of the pile of sand, and demolished it in the process, they jumped up from their knees and ran into the cold sea and swam about for a bit before they plunged to shore on a wave and shook out their hair, and Ben jumped the breakwater and ran on down the long beach, and Rose plodded back just in time to put a cotton dress over her swimsuit and take up some of the morning teas.

The running was so good and cleansing, but still the anxiety ran with her, of a piece of knowledge just beyond her grasp, something that still had to be done.

When Mr Vingo came back unexpectedly in the middle of a wet night, coming down to breakfast next morning as if he had never been away and the new guest at his table was an old acquaintance, Rose asked him straight out. No fooling about with it. No time to waste. He had hinted before that he knew more than he revealed. Now he must tell her.

It was still raining mistily. The lounge and the verandah were full of squabbling children, and guests reading and doing jigsaw puzzles, so Rose and R. V. Vingo went for a walk in the wood, off the path among the trees, where it was drier.

Rose told him. She had wondered how she would do it, but it was easy. She told him and he listened, as if she were describing a shopping trip to London.

'Yes . . . yes.' He stopped and leaned against a tree and turned down the brim of his blue hat, and looked down at Rose from under it with pride. 'I told you it was time now. You didn't want to believe it, but now you know.'

'It's all so confusing. What do I know?'

'That you are chosen to be a messenger of the grey hero.'

'*The horse?*'

He nodded solemnly.

'Why me?'

'That's never really made quite clear.' He shrugged. 'Because of this time of your life, and because of something – something in you.' He smiled at her. 'Something special. It isn't everyone.'

'I wish it wasn't me.'

'Oh no, you don't.' He looked shocked.

'I was scared, going down into the valley. The mist was so thick, and there were shapes of people moving, and voices. Men swearing and laughing.'

'So they know about you.'

'Who?'

'The soldiers of the Lord of the Moor.'

'But they're dead long ago.'

'In the valley, you're separated from time, exposed, like a crab without a shell. And where there's a power for good, there will always be forces of evil, struggling to prevail. Whatever shapes they take, he'll protect you from them, as long as you obey.'

'I don't know that I want to. I don't know that I want to be – what you said – a messenger.'

'You can't choose.' He had told her that before. 'But even if you could, wouldn't you choose glory?'

'Glor-ee!' Rose was excited. The memory of being on the horse's back, of the power of his flight and the roaring of the wind sent her running ahead, winding in and out among the trees with her arms out, touching their branches to shake off the drops of mist, weaving back to run a circle round Mr Vingo as he walked slowly, prodding at soggy dead leaves with his thick walking stick, and to ask him, 'Who is he then – the horse? Who is he?'

'I told you.'

'I don't know what to call him.'

'His name is Favour. Of all the horses at the castle, he was the strongest and swiftest and became the favourite of the Lord of the Moor.'

'But listen.' Rose stopped him. As they stood facing each other under the dripping trees, she put out her hands and held his arms through the damp grey coat. 'Why is he here, on this moor, in that valley?'

'This is his place.' Mr Vingo's words were short, because he was short of breath. 'And the legend happened here.'

'What?'

'Flood. Wicked Lord cut down trees for money. Nothing to hold river banks. Houses swept away. People would have

74

gone with 'em, but Favour raced the flood waters to warn them.'

'Where is the valley now?'

'Under the lake.'

'So it's not really there.'

'For you, it is.'

'But I can't find it now.'

'You will.' He winced because Rose was gripping his arms.

'Sorry.' She let go of him and stepped back, and he brought the handle of his ash plant up to the brim of his hat, and threw out his heaving chest.

'I salute you, messenger of the grey horse.'

Rose bowed.

Either he was mad, or she was.

Above them, at the tops of the trees, the rain seemed to have stopped, and Mr Vingo said it was time to go home. They walked slowly along the path. He was too out of breath to talk, so Rose told him some more about the old man and his poor crazed wife, and Felicity and her mother in the fur hat.

'So what does it mean, a messenger? Am I supposed to take a message back to them? I wasn't any help to them. I can't change what became of their lives. It's too late.'

'Never too late to stop that happening to other people. You understand that?'

'No.'

'Nor can I really.' He laughed.

She opened the gate for him, and as they went through the back garden, she pulled him over to the fence to look across at the back of the annexe.

'Looks nice, doesn't it?'

The sun was blinking through clouds in a watery way, and a child jumped down the steps from the glass doors and ran in circles, making silvery tracks on the wet grass.

'Charming.'

'I think it's haunted.'

'Who by?' He rested his arms on top of the board fence and put his chins on his hands.

'The two old people? They were so unhappy.'

'They're part of it perhaps. I don't know. You have to find the clue.'

'Clue to what?'

'I don't know.'

'Don't keep *saying* that. You know more than me.'

'No,' he pivoted his large head from side to side on his hands.

'What am I supposed to do?'

'I don't – 'He looked at her guiltily, put his hands over his mouth and started to cough.

'I can't understand,' said Rose. 'They were quite ordinary, decent people, if you think about them, but something wouldn't let them be like that. Something about the house – could that be it?'

Mr Vingo was walking away from her back to the hotel, his shoulders hunched, his hands over his face, coughing.

The house. She turned to frown at its lively back windows, gay with coloured curtains, a bright swimsuit on one of the sills, a young woman leaning out to call to the child.

It seemed to bring out the worst in them.

CHAPTER EIGHT

The next time Rose heard the tune, she was trotting along on Moonlight.

Her riding had improved. 'Wonders will never cease!' Joyce shouted in her flattering way. She was sitting more still and firmly. Moonlight was not falling over his large feet so often, because she was not losing her balance and tipping forward nervously.

'Rose Wood!' Joyce roared across the muddy field where they were jumping infinitesimal fences that most of the horses knocked down out of boredom. 'I see hope for you at last!'

Well, no wonder, after what had happened to Rose. Hadn't she ridden Horse of all Horses in a flying gallop? Moonlight was tame stuff after that.

Because Joyce was so mellow today, and was sporting a small diamond on her left hand to show that her young man had finally got up enough nerve to propose, she allowed Rose half an hour extra to take Moonlight up to the moor and see if she could make him canter. 'And for God's sake, don't let him put his head down and eat grass.'

Moonlight did not particularly want to canter. That was all right. His five-legged canter twisted you like a corkscrew. Rose was happy to trot steadily along, singing to the muffled drum beats of his hoofs on the turf. She sang, '*Chicks* and *ducks* and *geese* better *scurry, when* I *take* you *out* in the *surrey,*' which was a good song for a trot. '*When* I take you out in the surrey with the fringe – on *top*.' Her voice went up. '*Ther* wheels are yaller – ' Her voice squeaked. It would not come down.

It had risen into the upward spiralling notes of that special tune. She was singing words she did not know, as the tune filled her head. She turned Moonlight with difficulty and kicked him into his ungainly canter, up a slope, recklessly down the other side and across a stony stretch, with her eyes fixed ahead to where she could see in the distant haze the grey rock, waiting like a sentinel.

Before she reached it, Moonlight stopped abruptly and put his head down to graze, and she slid off down his neck.

It was all there, the mist, the ground dropping away, the vague moving shadows, but she shut her eyes and struck out to keep them away from her sliding, headlong descent to the stream – and Favour! He appeared in a dazzle of light and energy, waiting impatiently for her to climb up the other side to him.

She did not hesitate. She had to go to him, but when he turned his head to look at her with a full and shining eye, she was afraid and had to look away. What was she doing? The valley dropped steeply below her. She tried to step back against the rock wall, but her feet moved forward, and she was on his back, and the soaring, incredible flight bore her away.

'It's time to go!'

'Not ready!'

As she ran upstairs, two at a time, away from the small child's voice, she saw that her feet wore black patent leather shoes with straps, and her stockings were made of cotton.

'Sylvia!' The child's voice from below, whining. 'Sylvi-er! Me and Jack want to go to the party.'

'You wait, you rotters,' Sylvia called down over the bannisters, which Rose realized were the bannisters at Wood Briar: an oak rail, rounded to fit your hand, or your bottom if you were sliding down. Sylvia went on up into her room, one of the hotel bedrooms, but it did not have the neat, functional hotel furniture, with the chintz bedspreads Mollie had bought for all the rooms this year – this year, which year? where was she now? – nor the notice by the light switch about meals and departure time.

Sylvia's clothes were strewn about: a kilt, a school gym tunic, a green blazer with a gaudy badge on the pocket. On the bed were a crinoline doll and a harlequin and a pile of fluffy toy animals. Shoes and a tennis racquet spilled out of the open wardrobe door, on the back of which were tacked up pictures of horses from magazines, with jockeys on them and men standing about in silly tweed hats and knickerbockers, and flat-shaped women in hats like flowerpots, low over the eyes.

In the mirror, Sylvia was rather flat too. She wore a restricting kind of garment that made her the same shape all the way down the front to the patent leather belt of her straight dress, worn very low, miles below the waist. The front of her bobbed hair was looped over to the side and held with a daisy clip. She was ready to take her younger brother and sister to the party next door, but she didn't want to go.

She did not dislike the family there. She hardly knew them, since they had not been there long. But she did not like anyone at the moment, because her mean, rotten parents would not let her have a pony, and everything here was done for those silly little ones, and there was nothing to do in this God-forsaken place to which her family had moved five years ago because Sylvia had had tuberculosis and the air was said to be salubrious.

My fault again. Sylvia tugged the belt lower, until it was almost down to the hem. Always my fault.

All this Rose knew as it passed through Sylvia's head, while she hitched up the cotton stockings, which had bits of elastic tied round the top, and chewed at her lips to make them pinker, because her old-fashioned mother would not let her wear the orange lipstick that everyone at school had gone wild for.

There was a battering on her door, and she jerked it open and made a terrible frightening face at Daphne and Jack, anxiously hopping about in their party clothes outside.

'Come on, hurry up,' she said. 'Catch me if you can!' She hurtled past them to the stairs, slid down the bannisters to land with a thump in the hall, and dodged out of the door to the verandah before they could see where she went.

She ran along the echoing boards and climbed over a wicker screen to the side verandah, where she vaulted the rail and dropped into the garden. Crouching low, she scuttled among shrubs to the summer house and slid across its red tile floor to hide behind the folded deck chairs.

The little ones had come out of the house and were mewing about on the lawn. 'Sylvi-er! Silly Syl! We'll tell our mother!'

She waited until they were near the summer house and then pounced out, sending them into screams, which changed to shrieks and giggles as she rolled them over and tickled them, messing up their party clothes.

She was soon sick of it. *'Small pleasures of life are fleeting and trivial,'* she quoted to herself from one of her own poems, retied Daphne's sash, brushed down Jack and wiped his disgusting nose, and took them firmly in each hand. *'O, gentle sister, little mother.'*

They walked round to the front and primly along the road to the house next door, and primly up the brick walk of the garden, newly planted with roses and flowering rhododendrons. Doris, the maid, opened the door and smiled at them, which was unusual. When she visited the maids at Sylvia's house, she depressed the kitchen with her grumblings about the 'dreadful hole' of her situation. The house looked gayer than usual, because it was Sonny's birthday party. There were balloons and paper streamers

The maid opened the door . . .

M.—D

and fairy lights, and a jolly uncle in a paper hat and false nose, and an aunt who banged on the piano for musical bumps, and the dining-room table was spread with sandwiches and cakes and crackers and little paper cups of jelly.

Sonny's parents told Sylvia to leave her present in the study at the back. The father was supposed to be something to do with newspapers. There were some framed cartoons on the wall with grotesque black and white people with huge noses and endless legs, saying things in balloons. Rose saw that he was a short, square man, and his wife was tall, with long thin fingers on which a heavy carved ring . . .

My God! Rose metaphorically clapped a hand to her head, although she had no head or hand except those belonging to Sylvia, who was turning over the presents to see how theirs compared. *My God, the ring!* This was the old cartoonist and his wife at a much earlier age – fifty – sixty years ago.

Before the afternoon got cold, there was a treasure hunt in the orchard where the apple blossom lay under the trees as if they had stepped out of pink and white petticoats, Sylvia thought. The ornamental cherry was still full out, and she went and lay under it and looked up through a foam of fragrant pink, as if she were seeing the sky through soap. She did not know, as Rose did, that in fifty or sixty years the tree would be fallen and dead.

Sylvia was the oldest one here, except for the grown-ups. She had only come to bring Jack and Daphne, because her mother was in the hospital, having another baby, for some reason. Other people's mothers were here and some nannies, uniformed and clucking in a bunch together, or bending over the pram of the baby of the house, Joan, crooning and saying, 'Isn't she a darling!', to cover their professional criticism of clothes, make and probable cost of pram, colour of cheeks, size for her age, etc.

The Mumford twins were also objects of attention, although heaven knew they left a lot to be desired, but they took advantage of being twins. They were identical five-year-olds, dressed alike, and rather blank and pudding-faced. When Sylvia asked them who was who, for something to say, they slid their small eyes sideways at each other under their thick lids and said, 'I'm Angela,' and, 'I'm Audrey,' in a way that made you think they were not.

At tea, the twins were not allowed to sit together, because their mother had been reading a new book which said that twins had to be independent. One of them pretended to see a white cow outside the window and screamed.

'Strong imagination,' her mother said.

'Playing for attention,' the nannies muttered.

The twin at the end of the table pressed her lips together and made a scared face, and behaved rather strangely, and would not eat.

The mothers and nannies standing round the room behind the children clucked, and discussed in whispers whether Mrs Mumford was wrong or right.

Sylvia stood against the wall too, refusing to be classed as a child, and pretended not to be hungry. She would be having supper with Daddy after the babies were in bed. Actually she ate quite a lot, which was nice for Rose, but she had to go home to fetch a cardigan, because Daphne was cold in the dining-room, and by the time she came back, tea was over.

After the meal, the party flagged a bit, as parties do, so the jolly uncle called for Hide and Seek, and switched the false nose round on its elastic to the back of his head, to make people laugh.

The lights went out. The children scattered. The birthday boy went into the study with the grown-ups and hid his face in the leather armchair and began to count to fifty.

Sylvia went into the kitchen to talk to Doris. The kitchen had been done up, with new wood cabinets and a fancy floor of marbled linoleum. Sylvia finished the left over orange jellies and dried some plates for Doris, and dropped one with a crash as there was a terrible screaming from somewhere in the house, and the sound of running feet.

The lights were turned on. The grown-ups were babbling. 'What happened? Is someone hurt? I never trust Hide and Seek.' Children frightened by the noise came down from upstairs and hid their faces in their mothers' clothes.

Out of the dining-room was carried one of the Mumford twins, not screaming now, but white as suet, sobbing and trembling and unable to talk.

'What's the matter?'

Mrs Mumford didn't know. The other twin didn't know. She had been made to go and hide upstairs while her sister stayed down.

Sonny said, 'She was hiding in the cupboard. I knew she was there, but I didn't go to look, cos it's not fair to find the babies too soon.' (He was a year older.)

'What frightened her?'

'Dunno.'

'There's nothing in there – look!' The jolly uncle waltzed in and out of the deep dining-room cupboard where the shelves were full of plates, with his false nose on the back of his head, but the petrified Mumford twin would not be reanimated. Even a spoonful of brandy did not revive her. She dribbled it back down her mother's front, and had to be wrapped in a blanket and taken home.

The party began to break up. Mothers and nannies gathered up their children and dressed them in coats and outdoor shoes and put their party slippers into shoe bags. Everyone said, 'I had a lovely time, thank you.'

The birthday boy was disappointed. His mother said,

'People always go home too early,' and the father looked at her rather nastily and said, 'Whose fault, I wonder?'

While Daphne and Jack were looking for their cracker prizes, Sylvia, who was inquisitive because she was going to be a writer, went to try to see what had frightened the Mumford twin. Rose, who had to go with her, kept saying, 'Don't! Don't!', screaming at her silently not to go into the cupboard, but Sylvia opened the door and went inside.

'Don't shut the door!'

But she pulled the door shut and stepped into a blackness of fear that dropped Rose down and down, falling into a bottomless black pit in which there was no end of falling.

With a jerk that made her heart lurch, Rose opened her eyes to find herself spreadeagled on the turf of the moor, flat on her back, as if she had been dropped there from a great height. Above her the sky, and something else. Something moved near her hand, and she pulled it away just before Moonlight trod on it. His square white nose and pink lips came down to check her over. She jumped up and hugged him for not leaving her and going back to the stable.

He had put his foot through one of the reins and broken it. Rose tied the broken end to the bit, and he found his way back to the path and took her back to the stable, with her head aching and a taste of orange jelly in her mouth.

'I *told* you not to let him put his head down,' Joyce fussed at her.

'I'll pay to have it mended.'

'That's not the *point*.'

'Sorry I've been so long.'

'You haven't. I didn't expect you to be back so soon, but I suppose this cunning old devil –' she slapped Moonlight so hard that he staggered – 'said to himself, "Enough's enough".'

'I suppose.'

'Are you all right? You didn't fall off or anything, did you?'

'No,' Rose said, like a child leaving a party. 'I had a lovely time. Thank you.'

What was she supposed to do *now*? Favour was so mighty that Rose hardly dared to think about him in her real life, but she could not help wishing he would be a bit more definite about what he wanted. A messenger, Mr Vingo said. Messenger of the grey horse. But to carry what messages where?

Clues, Mr Vingo said. This time, the clue was obvious. She had needed to puzzle out that the Felicity episode showed that there was something in the house that brought out the worst in people's natures; but the significance of the birthday party was easy. There was something wrong with that cupboard. Well, she knew that before she went all those years back in time, to Sonny's birthday. She had never really believed those comfortable explanations for why the cupboard door would not stay shut: it was damp, the floor wasn't level.

Brings out the worst in people . . . Jake and Julie. Rose had never known them to quarrel before. They had been back to the hotel once, since the time she found Julie crying in bed in the annexe, and they had stayed in their favourite Room Four in the hotel and been their old selves.

The annexe did not affect everybody, however. It seemed to have its ups and downs. At the moment it housed two families with children, who were friends. They made their own breakfasts and picnic lunches, and said that it was as good as having their own holiday house.

Jim Fisher had wrenched his shoulder, so Ben, who was working his body hard and wanted to be outdoors all the time, was mowing the back lawn for Mollie.

Crossing the garden on her way to the annexe, Rose was

not going to talk to him, because if he stopped the motor of the mower it could be hard to start, but he yelled at her over the noise, and she went over.

'When's lunch?'

'Not for ages.'

'Damn.'

He moved away from her. Rose realized that she was standing somewhere near the place where Sylvia had hidden in the summer house. There had never been a summer house in Rose's time, and the flowering shrubs were gone, and the cramped little gravel paths and box hedges, but, as far as she could tell, this was about the place where Sylvia had slid in to hide from Daphne and Peter. Now there was only sweet-smelling mown grass, a bit flatter than usual because Ben had been rolling it.

If there had never been a summer house, then perhaps it was all a dream, and Mr Vingo was deranged.

She went into the annexe to collect towels and tidy up a bit. Opening the front door to shake out the mat, she remembered how nice the front garden had looked when Sylvia, 'gentle sister, little mother,' came up the path in her patent leather shoes – mauve and white rhododendrons and deep pink roses. Must talk to Mollie about planting roses for next year. Rose would buy her a rose bush for her birthday. And plant it. And bring a bucket of manure from Moonlight's stable to nourish it.

In the kitchen, she found that the families had tidied up after themselves, instead of, like some guests, leaving dirty breakfast things all over the place, and flies getting into the milk, which bore out Mrs Ardis's prophecy that they would all live to regret the day that they let the gorillas loose with food. Mrs Ardis thought of the paying customers as if they came from a zoo, and always expected the worst.

The refrigerator did not have any messy scraps of butter or hard ends of cheese or souring mugs of milk the baby wouldn't drink. There was some bread and ham and some mustard, so Rose slapped together a sandwich for Ben and went to the fence and waved it at him.

He stopped the mower and ran into the annexe, his forehead under the short curls glistening with sweat. His long legs and arms were very brown this year.

'Snack time.' Rose poured him a glass of lemonade and he sat down at the table with the sandwich, and she stood over him like a woman in a television commercial, watching her husband eat margarine that tasted like butter.

'Sit down,' Ben said. 'Take the weight off your feet. You work too hard.'

'There's a lot to do. I like it.'

'What do you do for fun?'

'Well – you know. I ride. Go on the beach.' She did not say, 'I run with you,' because perhaps that was supposed to be serious.

'They work you too hard.' He bit into the sandwich, wrinkling his damp forehead. 'Child labour, it used to be called.'

'But Ben, I love it. Plus I get money. It's my life, but it can't be for ever. My mother and I, we have a sort of pact between us that when I get sick of it, I'll say so, and she'll hire three other people to do what I do.'

'Child labour. She could be prosecuted.'

'Don't talk about my mother like that.' Rose was not angry, but sad that he did not understand the partnership between her and Mollie.

'Sorry. I just felt – sort of bloody-minded.'

'It's because you got too hot out there, and you're eating too fast.'

'Yes, mother.'

Rinsing his glass at the sink, she laughed, because she thought he was joking, but when she turned round he looked angry.

'I didn't mean . . .' She had said the wrong thing again.

He got up, wiped his mouth with the back of an oily hand, and went out.

She heard him trying to start the mower half a dozen times, which must be making him even angrier. She listened until the engine caught and roared, then picked up her laundry bag of towels and went back to the hotel. As she was going in at the back door, she heard a sudden loud clunk, and the mower stopped, and then Ben swore and kicked angrily at something in the grass at the edge of the lawn. Rose put down the bag and went over to him. His face was flushed, as he squatted by the mower with a piece of the blade in his hand.

'Broke it right off. I never saw the thing.'

The corner of a chunk of buried stone was sticking up under the grass. It was one of the red tiles from the floor of Sylvia's summer house.

CHAPTER NINE

The Mumfords did not visit in the summer, except once a
month when Mollie and Hilda and Mollie's friend Samson,
who gave cooking lessons in the village, put on a big buffet
for Sunday lunch. Extra tables were put out on the porch,
and it was advertised in the paper, so outside people came as
well as the hotel guests. The Mumfords came, with greedy
eyes, making two or three trips back to the buffet to get
their money's worth.

'Probably don't eat for a week afterwards,' Philip Wood
said. He helped with the lunches, pouring wine and beer
and being quite debonair, so that Rose and Mollie hoped
that he might in the end take to the hotel business, but he
always disappeared before Sam brought out the fruit and
cheese and the pastries he had made, and if he enjoyed it, he
never let on.

Sometimes Rose wanted to take him and shake him and
tell him, 'Love life!' But she had other things on her mind
just now. She wanted to talk to the Mumfords.

She cornered them in the hall as they were going out to
their car.

'Remember what you said about the annexe,' she said,
standing between them and the open front door.

'Having trouble with it, are you?' one of them asked
hopefully. They were no taller than Rose, although she was
still short for her age.

'No, it's a great success. People love it.'

'That's good,' the other Miss Mumford said glumly, and
belched a little. She patted her mouth. 'Was that a different
brand of pickle?'

'Remember when you said about the birthday party?'

'What birthday party?' the one with the shaky head asked. 'We haven't celebrated our birthday for years, ha ha. When you get to our age, dear, you'll find out –'

Rose could not hang around while they went through all that 'Wait till you're my age,' and 'In my day . . .', which passed for conversation with some old people. 'You cried,' she said to shaky-head, 'when you were playing hide and seek.'

'Who said we played hide and seek?' the other Mumford asked suspiciously.

'Well, I mean, they always play hide and seek at birthday parties.'

'I dare say.' They closed their faces. What would they say if Rose addressed them as Audrey and Angela?

'Did you hide in a cupboard?'

'My dear child, don't keep prattling on like this when we want to go. We don't remember a thing about it, and that's that. When you get to our age . . .'

She let them go. They drove away like toy figures, upright in a small sky-blue car. The one who did not shake drove, her head hardly high enough to see over the wheel.

'They said they couldn't remember,' she told Mr Vingo.

'Just as well. You mustn't try to tell people your secrets.'

'I wasn't. I wanted to find out whether any of it really happened, or whether it was a dream, or my imagination.'

'Do you seriously doubt?'

'It's all too weird. Things like this don't happen. Not to me, they don't. I'm ordinary.'

'You're special.' He sighed. 'When will you get that through your stubborn head, Rose of all the world?'

They were in his room because he had offered to help her with her piano practice, but he was sitting on the piano stool, not Rose. He swung round and played the melody

91

from the ballet *Spectre de la Rose,* and forced his voice to sing about the rose that the girl wears to her first ball, which comes back in the night to dance with her: '*Je suis la spectre de la ro-ose, que tu-u po-or-tai-ais hier au bal.*' His voice cracked. 'But that girl was asleep during her strange experience. You weren't.'

'I wasn't last night, I know that. I was awake all night, worrying about what it all means.'

'You're a hard worker. You shouldn't be daunted by a job.'

'Except I don't know what the job is.'

'To find the way back. Where there is unhappiness and unrest, your mission as a messenger of the Great Grey Horse is to follow the threads back and back and back to whatever tragedy of the past has left this haunting legacy.'

'And then do what?'

'Resolve it.'

'Golly.' Rose digested this. She frowned. 'How do you know?'

R. V. Vingo gave a little modest laugh. 'I was a messenger once.'

'You!'

'I was your age once, incredible though it may seem. As a matter of fact –' he looked at his hands, plump under the fingertips from playing the piano – 'I still feel your age. That's one of the nice things, you'll find, about getting old.'

'Who else was a messenger?'

'Dozens of people all down through history; some good, some not so hot. Take the famous Blanche Orlando, for instance. She was said to have raised a man from the dead, but she let herself be exploited for money, as a medium on the Victorian stage, and lost her powers, and enraged Favour. Take silly Hugh, the village idiot, a man of fifty with a child's mind. He broke the spell of the Blind Baron, who lured maidens to his ghastly underground retreat, where they plucked out their eyes for him, in terror of what they saw. Take Leo of Pilot Rock. Wherever they are, in place or time, the horse finds 'em.'

'Suppose they don't want to be found?'

'Tough luck. They can't avoid it. You can't avoid it, Rose of all roses, by trying to make out it's all dreams or imagination.'

He swivelled his wide haunches round on the stool and began to play the lilting tune, and Rose thought, *Oh my God, not now, please, I'm too tired. Not ready. Afraid.*

Mr Vingo laughed, and switched to playing the march from his musical epic, the call to arms that roused the soldiers of the Lord of the Moor to ride out to join the king's army, with the proud grey horse at their head. He bent over the piano and breathed heavily at the part where the swing of it slowed to the monotonous drum, drum, drum of the night march home with the bodies they carried secretly back to the castle for the Lord to use in his ghastly experiments with the souls of dead men.

When Rose went up with tea next morning, he was gone. His bed was unmade and everything was strewn about as usual – his patent medicines and boxes of biscuits and mustard and cress in a saucer of blotting paper on the window sill.

They had got used to Mr Vingo as a fixture, and departing summer guests had begun to say to him, 'See you next year.' But today he was gone again in his mysterious way, and Rose's father began to speculate that R. V. Vingo was an enemy agent.

He had left a note for Mrs Ardis to lock his door and leave the key at the front desk, because last time his custard cream biscuits had gone while he was away.

Mrs Ardis puffed out the front of her flowered overall, blew upwards at a bit of hair that was hanging in her eyes and said, 'I have never been accused of anything like this, Mrs Wood, never.'

'He wasn't accusing you. But the hotel is full and there are a lot of children.'

Mrs Ardis said, 'Custard creams are bad for you. I eat only wheatmeal.'

She locked Mr Vingo's room but left the key in the door, as a sign of something or other.

Running on the beach, Ben said to Rose one morning, 'I didn't know you could play the piano so well.'

'I can't.'

'I heard you playing last night.' When they talked while they were running, they talked ahead, not looking at each other.

'When?'

'After I went to bed.'

'Where?'

'There's only one piano. In Mr Vingo's room.'

'Not me. He must be back.'

'Mm-mm.' Ben shook his brown head and raced ahead of her, his feet making clean tracks in the damp sand of last night's high tide.

Later that day, Rose was in the garden, picking zinnias and larkspur for the dining-room. Bare feet thudded along the boards, and Ben appeared on the side verandah and jumped over the rail and said to Rose, 'Listen.'

She straightened up and put her head on one side.

'Mr Vingo's piano.'

She heard it. 'He must be back.'

'He's not, I tell you. Let's go up and see who it is.'

'No.' Rose felt afraid.

'What's the matter, little girl?'

When Ben called her that, she wanted to punch him. Instead she followed him up the back stairs and along the empty corridor. As they reached the end by the winding stair to the turret, Rose stopped.

Someone was playing *that* tune on the marmalade piano.

'Come on.' Ben turned and saw her face. 'What's up?'

'That tune.'

'What tune? Whoever it is, they're playing scales.'

'No, that tune. Mr Vingo played it at the concert. You heard it, like a flute, just before I left. Listen. There it is again.'

Ben looked blank. He had not heard the tune before. He could not hear it now.

Step by step, Rose was drawn forward, going past Ben to climb the stairs ahead of him to the turret room. The music had stopped. The door was locked. The key was on the outside.

Ben put out his hand. 'Let's go in,' he said, but he did not turn the key. Rose could not have gone into that room. Nor could Ben.

As they went down the stairs backwards, to keep an eye on the door and the steps above them, the piano started and Rose heard the clear notes of the tune again.

'Ben,' she said, 'there's a place I've got to go to. I want you to come with me.'

She did not want to go alone this time, and she wanted him to know. He thought she was the same Rose she'd always been. She wanted him to know that she was special, wanted him, if it was possible, to see what she had seen. Even though he had not heard the tune, he had heard the ghost of the piano.

'Come up to the moor?' she asked, her breath catching in her throat.

'Not for long. I've got tennis. What's the matter?'

'I'm afraid.'

'Me too.' He glanced back at the stairway. 'I'm afraid we're schizo. We've been hearing things. No piano now,' he said.

But there *was*. Its notes were in her ears and head.

'Come and run.' She turned and sped down the back

stairs and out into the garden and through the wood, with Ben's feet pacing just behind her.

He said once, 'Is this a race?' and laughed, but then they ran in silence, steadily, across the pasture and over the wall, up and down small hills, zigzagging on the sheep track. Rose's breath was gasping and sobbing.

'Far enough,' Ben said. 'Turn back and slow down. Walk a bit.'

But they were coming to the huge grey rock that stood sentinel to the trees. Rose stopped. 'This is the place,' she gasped. Panting, she turned her face to breathe into the wind, as Ben had taught her. Breathing easily, he leaned against the rock and crossed his legs. Leaning on the rock seemed to Rose somehow disrespectful, like leaning against the bulk of Mr Vingo.

When she could speak, she said, 'Come on,' and led him beyond the rock to the path through the trees and the mists of the valley. There was no valley there. Only the quiet waters of the little lake, ringed by bushes and trees that dipped their heavy summer branches towards the water.

'So what?' Ben said. 'Noah's Bowl.'

'There used to be a valley here, ages ago. A flood filled it in.' Rose spoke fast to keep his attraction. 'Over there – you can't see it now – it drops down past farms and cottages to a tiny little fishing village. And you – and you see, the valley is here sometimes, I've seen it, and it's all misty and shapes moving about, because once long ago there was this wonderful horse who –'

'A horse. You've got this neurotic thing about horses. Thank God boys don't go through that stage.'

'But I saw him, Ben.' She had to make him understand. 'The horse.'

'Hears a piano. Sees a horse,' he grumbled. 'Brings me all this way. Your imagination's gone beserk, Rosie.'

'You heard the piano.'

96

'It must have been someone's radio.'

'*We heard it.*'

'Give it a rest, little girl,' he said in that fifteen-year-old way that made her want to hit him. 'You'll grow out of it. It's all nonsense.'

It was easier to agree with him than to be angry. 'All right, then,' she said. 'I suppose it is.'

She took a step back, away from him, and, with a thunderous roar as the water receded, the ground rumbled and shook and parted into the cleft of the valley. The mist swirled in, and she stumbled down the slope to where it should have cleared to brightness, but it was dark at the bottom of the valley, as if the sun had gone down, the bridge in shadow, the river surging swollen and sluggish round the stones. Only the horse above her on the other side was a dazzle of light, shaking off sparks of cold fire as he raged at her and stamped and shook his head, his curved ears laid back.

Behind and around her in the clinging mist was the murmur of voices, the coarse laughter and the chink of steel and rasp of a boot on stone.

'Help me!' But she had denied the horse, and he turned away his head and stared down the valley. He had called her, but she did not obey, and so he would not protect her, a crab without its shell. She tried to move towards him, but cold fingers plucked her back. Her feet were lead. A soldier laughed in her face with a stench of foul breath, and she swayed and fell, and her senses reeled into blackness.

She woke with the roaring of water in her ears, lying on her back on the wet grass at the edge of the lake. Her clothes were wet and her hair straggled over her face. Ben was leaning over her.

'What . . ?'

'You stumbled and fell into the water. I had to pull you out.'

'Did you see?'

'I saw you with your head in the air, not looking where you were going. As usual.'

'Couldn't you see, in the mist . . ?'

'What mist? Your eyes want examining.' The hair on his bare arms was golden in the sunlight. 'You trip over a stone like a clot, and now look at you.'

He had taken off his shirt to dab a cut on her forehead. 'Look.' He showed her the blood. 'You must have hit your head on something under the water. You were knocked out for a minute. Too bad you came round. I was going to practise my resuscitation techniques on you. I've been longing to save someone.'

Rose stood up. 'I'm all right.'

'Are you sure? Listen, we've got to get back. I'll be late. Come on.'

She jogged a little way with him, deliberately going slowly, so that when he told her to keep up, she could say, 'You go on ahead. I'll be all right.'

He peered at her, dabbed at her forehead again, and left the shirt with her. 'Take it easy.'

When he was out of sight, she turned and ran back to the valley, which she knew would be there, waiting for her.

This time as she plunged down into the hateful mist, the cloaked figures were more distant and shadowy, and she knew that once she was out into the bright light within sight of Favour and on to the bridge, she was safe. A bridge between evil and good. She ran across the slippery planks, watching the horse carefully. He still seemed wrathful at her treachery, so she approached him this time with more dread, but there was no holding back. She had to climb up to where he was, and although his hoof stamped sparks out of the flinty rock, she clambered on to his back and clung desperately to his mane as he took off like a rocket.

The flight was faster and rougher than before, and less

exhilarating, like an uncoordinated ride on any wayward horse, which showed that the horse, for all he was a mighty hero, was still a horse. A man's voice began to vibrate through the rush of the swift air. Nervous of who it was and where she was going, Rose began to stutter to Favour, 'Wherever it – it – it is, I *will* do well for you!'

He was no longer there. The man's voice clarified, and she was hurrying across a polished floor, in a long skirt and felt slippers, because the voice sounded urgent. 'Sister! Sister!'

It was a young man's voice, hoarse and weak. In the front room, a dim lamp showed two other beds with sleeping men, and the young man who was calling, his head moving restlessly from side to side, his hands plucking at the red blanket.

'Sister? Oh, it's Evie. Hullo.' He gave an anxious smile. His face was terribly thin and pale, with a stubble of beard and dark shadows round his eyes.

'What do you want, Michael?' Evie put a hand on his hot forehead. She was wearing a grey cotton dress with a long white cuff over the sleeve. 'I'm not a real nurse yet, you know, but I can get Sister.'

'No – no don't. I just want to know someone's there.' He took her hand and held it. The other arm was bandaged. A humped frame under the bedclothes kept their weight off the stump where his leg had been amputated.

One of the men in another bed stirred and woke, groaned and rolled on to his back, and put up a hand for the large pocket watch which hung on a string from the bed rail. He held it to his eyes. 'After ten. She's late with my sleeping medicine.'

'You *were* asleep.'

'How could I be if I haven't had my medicine? Go and hurry her up, Evie, there's a dear good girl.'

Evie got her hand away from Michael's with difficulty and padded across the hall to the kitchen, where her mother, in a nurse's uniform, was heating milk on an old gas stove that Rose had never seen before.

'The sergeant wants his sleeping draught.'

Evie's mother laughed. She had big teeth and a puff of light red hair under her white cap. 'Doctor Bond has reduced it to almost nothing, but it will send him off like a baby.' She measured a meagre amount of brown liquid from a large bottle on a shelf and gave the small glass to Evie. 'Fill it up with water.'

Evie gave the sergeant his medicine. He swallowed it with a heave of his Adam's apple, said, 'Gaw bless yer' and went back to sleep. Evie went to Michael's bed and asked him, 'Are you all right?' He nodded, but when she took the glass out to rinse he followed her with his feverish eyes.

The kitchen was fitted up as if it was part of an old-fashioned hospital. The floor was scrubbed wood. Where the dark cabinets had been, there were shelves of bottles and pill boxes, rolled bandages, enamel bowls, big jars of ointment. Charts hung on a long nail. A big three-level trolley by the wall held metal trays and piles of china and cutlery.

Her mother wore a long grey dress with a stiff stand-up collar and a long apron with a starched white belt and a red cross on the bib. On her red hair, she wore a white cap with a turned-up brim. She and Evie were wearing felt slippers because they were on night duty. Evie was wearing a small version of the same uniform. She hooked a finger inside her stiff collar to ease it, and put her hands up to poke a pin back into the bun of long fluffy hair under her cap.

She looked round to see what she could do, because there was always something to do, and picked a bandage to roll out of the laundry basket, rolling it up in a practised way and smoothing it neatly against the front of her apron bib.

'I can't wait till you're old enough to be a nurse,' the mother said. 'If this endless war goes on through nineteen seventeen, and eighteen, and nineteen, and for ever, you will be.'

'I am a nurse, Mother,' Evie said.

'As good as. You're a great help now that they've taken so many nurses out of the convalescent hospitals to go to France. And I'd much rather have you here with me when I'm on night duty, than alone at the cottage.'

'Michael's not up to much tonight,' Evie said. 'Not up to much' was a favourite expression of the Sister in Charge for any man who was very ill or in pain.

'His wounds are mending.' Her mother looked sad. 'But his spirit is not.' The wide mouth that was always smiling round her big teeth was drawn in thoughtfully. 'They call it shell shock, and they say he'll get over it in time, but I don't know. His regiment was wiped out at the Battle of the Somme.' She looked at Evie sadly. 'You're so young to have to hear this, Evie, but you're part of this war. Thousands of men were killed in those few days of fighting. Uselessly killed, just to gain a few yards of land. Sent out from the trenches into the mud and shell holes and barbed wire of No Man's Land to be torn to bits by the German guns. That was where Michael got his leg wound, running forward, screaming at the guns. He had just seen his father blown to pieces.'

Evie was silent. Rose wondered how she could hear those things without crying. Her mother went out of the kitchen with a tray of medicines.

Evie stepped out into the garden to get some air. There was a smell of autumn, dampness and dead leaves, apples on the grass. Rose saw that many lights were on in the big house next door. The two houses were evidently part of the same hospital. There was a paved path between them, and no fence. At the end of the garden, she thought she saw out of the corner of her eye something white moving behind the trees. Favour? When she looked again, there was only darkness there.

She picked up an apple, looked at it for worms and bit into it, standing on the wet grass in her slippers and long blowing white apron. She thought about Michael seeing his father blown apart, and how you would never get that image out of your mind, and about her own father, who was somewhere at sea. They didn't know where. There was no news coming through. His last letter had been from Scotland, but that was weeks ago.

Evie was very tired. It was difficult to sleep in the day time, because she still had to go to school, which was senseless, with the War to End All Wars going on. She was supposed to sleep part of the night in a chair by the fire in the hall, but the house was full of the noises of the men: coughing and moans and voices calling, someone talking in his sleep, the rustle of her mother's feet and skirts going to and fro, Sister from the main hospital tap-tapping over the floors as she did her rounds (not in slippers), a convalescent man who could not sleep getting up for a cigarette, or to make tea in the kitchen.

She went indoors and laid up the trays on the trolley for breakfast: knife, fork, spoon, mug, plate, porridge bowl, salt, pepper. She cut mounds of bread and butter to help the day nurses, covered it with a damp cloth, and put the porridge on to stew for the rest of the night in the double boiler that could never be quite cleaned of its crust. Then her mother wanted her upstairs to hold Mr Carter's leg while she changed the dressing.

The lamp was lit over the bed. The rest of the room was in darkness. They were like people on a stage, a tableau of pain. The soldier had his head back and his teeth clenched, holding on to the rail of the bed. Evie held her breath and stuck out the tip of her tongue as she carefully supported the heavy leg, which was bleeding again, oozing dark blood from the swollen and discoloured skin. Her mother bent over, with fiercely intent eyes, quick, deft, catching her breath when she had hurt him.

'It's better, eh?' he asked her, without looking at the leg.

'I hope so, Mr Carter.' It was much worse, but she was not allowed to say so. She was only a V.A.D. – it stood for 'Voluntary Aid Detachment' – not a qualified nurse, and would never be allowed to change dressings if they were not so short of staff, in this most merciless year of the war, when the casualties came back from France in thousands.

She and Evie made their slippered rounds of the wards with the torch held low. Then they made cocoa and Evie dozed and woke and dozed in the chair, while her mother sat by the fire and mended pillowcases. The house was quiet. The clock ticked more loudly. The hall was in shadow beyond the circle of lamp and firelight. It was so strange to be the only ones awake, with all the sleeping men around them. It made you feel you were the hub of their world, totally responsible for them, because they were patients here, and the people in their lives outside, wives, parents, children, friends, had no connection with them.

We are their world . . .

The scream from the front room brought Evie awake in an instant. She jumped out of the chair and followed her mother to Michael's bed. He was leaning on his good elbow, staring and babbling, sweating and trembling with fear. As her mother tried to calm him, the upstairs buzzer shrilled. The men rang it for an emergency, so she had to go upstairs and leave Rose trying to push Michael's chest down, to keep him in the bed.

The sergeant came to her help. He got Michael to lie back and told him roughly, but kindly enough, to put a sock in it and let a bloke sleep.

'He had a nightmare, see,' he said to Evie, and went back to bed and pulled a blanket over his head.

Her mother came back looking anxious. 'Mr Carter's leg wound has broken down. I'll have to go over to the hospital and get the doctor. Can you manage? Evie will stay with you. Calm down, Mr Hunt.' As a nurse, she had to call him that. Only Evie could call him Michael to his face.

Evie sat on a hard upright chair by the bed. She heard the back door open and shut, and the voices of the doctor and the Scottish Sister, and their feet going upstairs.

'I dreamed of that man,' Michael kept whispering, 'that man, that man,' over and over, with his troubled eyes fixed on hers.

'A German?'

'I don't know. All in black, he was, he was . . .'

'Hush, it's all right. Don't talk about it,' Evie said, and Rose was glad, because his fear had made her afraid, and she wanted him to take his nightmare visions away from them, and go back to sleep. 'It's over now,' Evie told him. 'You're not at the war. Hush, Michael.' Sometimes she felt a hundred years old, and wondered where her youth had gone. 'It's only a dream.'

'Why do I have these terrible dreams?'

'It's the shell shock, isn't it? That's what they say. You'll be better soon, Michael. Go back to sleep.'

'Stay with me.'

'All right.' Evie turned her head away, so he would not see her yawn. She sat on the hard chair until he stopped gasping and shuddering and his grip on her hand loosened and his breathing grew more regular. It was cold. The window was open, and a damp sea smell was coming in. She yawned again and her legs moved restlessly because she was so tired. Rose had never felt so tired in her life – or anybody else's. She wanted to be out of this room of sickness and fear. Evie had done enough for Michael, surely. She and Rose – instead of only observing Evie, Rose felt very much a part of her – they could go back to the fire and be comfortable, and forget about all this.

The fire had died down, and she was too tired to fetch more coal. She put her mother's cape round her shoulders and picked up the sewing. With her mother still busy upstairs, Evie must stay awake and on guard. Rose thought she deserved a rest. She nodded and woke, listened for Michael, nodded and woke. After a while, the needle dropped and she could not find it in her skirt. The torn pillowcase dropped off her lap. She fell into a stupefied sleep, and Rose woke with a headache on the moor, trudging along the sheep track in a daze, trailing Ben's shirt behind her.

'Oh look at your head oh look at her head there's blood all over your forehead Rose we must get you cleaned up immediately Harry go and see where Mrs Wood is hurry Harry.'

'Come *on*, Mum.' Ben's young brother Harry pulled Mrs Kelly towards the door. She was wearing an alarmingly pink swimsuit with a brief skirt over it.

'But Rose needs help anyone can see that.'

'It's nothing,' Rose said. 'I'll wash it.'

'These things turn septic you know I knew a woman whose son tore his fingernail and before he knew it they had his hand off.'

'Give the girl a break,' Ben's father said. 'You'll give her a headache, if she hasn't got one already.'

Mr Kelly was a big, slow-moving man in square shorts and a beach jacket like a tent, who viewed his tearaway wife with amused tolerance.

'All of you don't care going off to the beach without a care in the world while poor Rose gets lockjaw because she does after all have a working mother not that I'm anti-feminist and we can't go into that argument about whether women should or shouldn't work when they have children.'

'Listen to her,' Mr Kelly said to nobody or anybody. 'She's bonkers.'

Rose went through the arch to the kitchen and the back stairs, keeping on the side of Hilda's dud eye. She washed her forehead in the bathroom upstairs and found a substantial cut. It bled again as she washed it. She thought of Mr Carter's terrible leg. She had never seen anything like that before.

She rolled Ben's bloodied shirt up into a ball and put it in a drawer. Her mother must have found it, because it was gone the next day. It was raining, so she did not know whether Ben would have asked her to run on the beach. He was staying away from her. She was too childish for him. Folding laundry with Cindy and only half listening to horror tales about the drug centre, she saw Cindy fold the shirt and put it on the ironing pile. Pity. It would have been nice to keep the shirt with her blood on it, after Ben was gone.

An old gentleman was staying in the hotel with a younger wife who was always off in the car, looking at the shops. Rose found him reading in the upstairs lounge and asked him, 'Excuse me. What was the Somme?'

'The worst battle of the First War.' His faded blue eyes looked up at her and blinked. 'A million men were killed on both sides.'

'I met a young man whose father was blown to pieces at the Somme,' Rose said.

'His great-grandfather, perhaps. If it was his father, he wouldn't be young now. He'd be as old as me.'

The television was on, because Gloria automatically flipped on the switch when she was not in the room, and left it on whether anyone was watching or not. The sound was turned low, so the old gentleman could not hear it as he read his book. It was a silly quiz show. A prattling host with big teeth like Evie's mother, but a fake smile and hard, glittering eyes, was giving away prizes to people who answered feeble questions, and squealed and jumped in the air and kissed the man with the teeth.

Rose watched for a few minutes in awful fascination. The camera zoomed in on the host, and he came right forward as if he were coming out of the set, and said with his synthetic smile, 'You failed.'

Rose looked to see which competitor was flouncing off the stage, pretending not to mind, but the man was talking to her.

'You failed.'

'I didn't,' she whispered, glancing at the old gentleman, who went on reading.

'You failed him.'

'Evie did.' Rose knew what he meant. 'She was tired.'

'*You* were tired.' He had a metallic, nasal voice, with a touch of phoney American. 'And cowardly. You thought she'd done enough.'

'I saw things I've never seen. I couldn't stand to see those men – the dreadful wound in that man's leg.'

He made a sound like 'phoo', and said, 'You didn't want to listen.'

'It was Evie who wouldn't let him talk about the dream,' Rose said breathlessly, feeling the same helpless panic she had felt by Michael's bed.

'*You* wouldn't listen to it.'

'I couldn't control what she did. Or Felicity. Or Sylvia.'

'Don't whine. Maybe you could. Wise up,' he said in his fake American. 'This is what it's all about.'

Rose could not speak.

'So what did you learn?' His teeth filled half the screen. His eyes glittered.

'Nothing.'

She could not look away. As she watched, his eyes became the dark grey eyes of the horse, glistening and sparkling with points of light, and his huge head filled the screen in a movement of flowing whiteness, and in his eyes she saw two of herself mirrored, with two arms up, as if to ward off a blow.

'Listen to this,' the old gentleman said behind her. 'It says in this book . . .'

She could not stay behind with him. She had to go with Favour. She had to go back with him, because she had failed him once, and this might be her last chance.

She followed her mother into the hospital kitchen, carrying a bag of postcards and toffees and things the men had asked her to buy for them. She hung her knitted coat in the cloakroom under the stairs and put on her white cap. She was surprised to see in the mirror that Evie had red hair, like her mother. Rose had always wondered what it would feel like to have red hair. Evie had sandy eyebrows and eyelashes too. And freckles.

Her mother reported for duty to the day nurse at her desk in the hall. She and Evie both wore stiff white cuffs, but as soon as the formalities were over, they took them off and set them on a shelf like inverted flower pots, and pulled on their long linen cuffs to work in. Rose wondered why they didn't roll up their sleeves, but this must be about seventy years ago, and so they didn't.

Evie went into the front room to give the sergeant his sentimental postcards, which he sent every day to his wife. On the chair by Michael's bed, a young girl was sitting, with her feet tucked under the chair rungs and a bunch of flowers in her lap. She and Michael both looked glum, as if they had been quarrelling.

'I'm just going,' she told Evie. 'I know it's after visiting hours.' She stood up, holding the flowers in a wrapping of newspaper. 'I'm not changing my mind, Mike,' she said, looking down at him with a face that was tender and determined at the same time. 'Please trust me. You aren't going to get rid of me.'

'Don't hang on, Clare,' Michael muttered without looking at her. His thin young face looked sulky. 'Go away, find someone else. I'll never be any use to you.'

'I'll come tomorrow.' She managed to smile at him.

'Here, I brought these flowers for you. Chrysanthemums. They're not very nice, I'm afraid. I stole them out of someone's garden along the road.'

She held them out to him, but he said, 'I don't want them. I can't stand the smell.'

'I know they're a bit past their prime, but –'

'They smell rotten.' He made a face. 'Sour. Take them away.'

'All right. Goodbye then, dear.' She bent to kiss him, but he turned his face aside. As she went out, Evie saw that she was trying not to cry. One of the yellow flowers dropped out of the newspaper and was left behind on the floor.

After lights out, when the white counterpanes were off and the red blankets tucked in, Evie asked her mother if she could stay in the room with Michael.

'I'm worried about him.'

'So am I, but I don't think you need to do that.'

'I think it's what I have to do,' Rose said in Evie's voice.

'All right, but do all the other jobs first. There are eleven men in this house, you know.' That was always the cry, even from Evie's mother, of tired, overworked nurses who suspected the men of playing for special attention.

When Michael fell restlessly asleep, Evie and Rose sat on the hard chair by his bed and listened to the sergeant snoring and the other man moaning in his sleep, and watched tense, fitful expressions alter Michael's face. He ground his teeth, and she saw his eyes move rapidly back and forth under the closed lids. He flung out an arm, and as Evie bent forward to calm him as he heaved and rolled over sideways with his head flung back and his mouth open, staring at the cupboard door on the other side of the bed.

His body went rigid and he screamed and opened his eyes. 'Look!' The outflung hand pointed at the closed door. 'Oh my God, my God . . .'

Evie turned on the light and tried to roll him back before

109

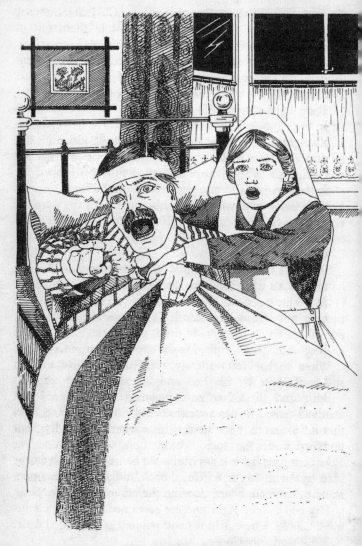

'Look!'

he hurt his wounded arm. 'It's all right, Michael, it's all right. I'm here.'

He flung himself on his back and lay staring up at her, panting and gasping, the cords in his neck standing out.

'Another nightmare. Poor Michael. There. Quiet now.' But tonight she did not say, 'It's only a dream.' She said, 'Tell me what it was.'

'In the cupboard.' He slid his eyes towards it. 'The man in black. He was hanging there. I had to go inside and it was all dark and I bumped into him and felt him swinging, and saw – I saw his face.'

So that was it. The cupboard. Rose had her answer. She could go back to her own time now, but there was Michael to be taken care of first.

'Stay with me.'

'Of course.'

She and Evie sat by him and comforted him and held his hand, and, in the lamplight, saw the tattered golden flower lying on the polished floor. As a faint grey light began to hover outside the window shades, Evie's eyes closed and she fell asleep.

Rose woke to find herself sitting peacefully in a chair in the hotel lounge, with the feel of Michael's thin hot hand still grasping hers.

Both times when Favour had taken her away for a night, she had looked at her watch when she returned and seen that it was not only the same time as when she had left, but the same date.

' . . . in this book it says,' the old gentleman was saying, 'that in the Antarctic Circle, the adelie penguin presents a stone to his mate when he wants her to make a nest.'

111

CHAPTER TEN

She was not going into that front room again. Doing beds in the annexe with Mrs Ardis, Rose ran upstairs and started on the top rooms, so that Mrs Ardis would start on the ground floor. But Mrs Ardis toiled up behind her. 'I'm not doing that great football field of a bed on my own. You'll have to help me.'

When they finished upstairs, Rose made an excuse to go back to the hotel, but Mrs Ardis grabbed her in the hall and said, 'One more bed to do, Miss Rose.'

'I haven't got time.'

'Then make time. What's the matter, Rose? You're so pale. Are you ill?'

Rose looked at the closed door of the front room and thought, *Yes, I am ill, with fear for myself and anybody else in this house, because in that room there is some dreadful secret terror that destroys people.*

'Mrs Ardis –' Because the chambermaid's pouchy eyes were looking at her quite kindly under the wild grey hair, Rose broke down and whispered, 'I'm afraid.'

'Afraid you're going to be sick? Nonsense,' said Mrs Ardis briskly. 'Hold it in; it's all in the mind. Come on, help me do that great ugly bed, and I'll make you some herbal tea.'

She opened the door of the front room and there was the bright bedroom, perfectly normal, swept and dusted for the next customers, a pile of clean sheets and towels on the bed.

It was Monday, the day they were supposed to turn all the mattresses. They did try, 'Because *She* expects us to.' Mrs Ardis referred to Mollie and Philip Wood disparagingly as '*She*' and '*He*', even in front of Rose.

112

'*She* is my mother.' Rose's fear made her irritable.

'That's your problem, Miss Rose, not mine.'

They heaved and puffed and got the unwieldy mattress on its side, but it fell heavily back again on top of Mrs Ardis. She struggled out from underneath it, looking as if she had been through a wind tunnel.

'A plague on it.' They left it and made up the bed. Rose stayed on the side away from the cupboard, and kept her eye on it. That was where Michael's bed had been. There was the sergeant's bed with its head to the window and the big watch on a string. Where the bed was now, on the new carpet, was where poor Clare's rejected flower had fallen on the polished floor.

'Mrs Ardis.' Rose tried again. 'You're psychic, aren't you? Could you tell if a place was haunted?'

'All places are haunted to me,' Mrs Ardis said unhelpfully, 'because I'm in tune with spirits from the past. They walk with me, converse with me, help me to bear a job like this which is so far beneath me.'

She threw on the flowered bedspread like a bullfighter with a cape, and as Rose settled it and smoothed it down, she saw to her horror that where it hung down on the side, one of the golden chrysanthemums was not looking upwards to the sun, like all the other flowers. It was drooping downwards, its petals wilting and ragged, like the yellow flower that had fallen on the floor when Clare left Michael.

What did that mean? Was that a sign for Rose? '*What am I supposed to do?*' she cried silently to the horse. But he had never given her any answers. She was the messenger. She was supposed to find the answers.

As she was tidying up in the annexe lounge, a car stopped outside, and Rose opened the door to two American women with suitcases and scarlet raincoats. Mollie had walked across the garden to meet them.

'This is your room,' she said. 'Number 1A. Our very best.'

'Oh, it's lovely,' the thin woman said.

'And this is my daughter Rose, who helps me.'

'She's lovely too.' Rose blushed. She wasn't. 'Let's stay for weeks and weeks. For a fortnight.'

They both laughed. It amused Americans to discover that two weeks was called a fortnight.

The chunky one sat down on the bed and started bouncing happily, her stocky legs over the wilted flower, as if nothing were amiss. Couldn't she see? Couldn't she feel? Why was it only Rose who knew something was wrong? 'Perfect,' the American said. 'Mrs Wood, I don't know how you do it for the money.'

'Nor do I.' Mollie laughed. Phil was always on at her to put the prices up as high as the other hotels, but she was afraid that people she liked might not come.

'They love it.' She came contentedly into the kitchen, where Rose was now sweeping out crumbs from under the table. This was the place where the big trolley had stood when it was a hospital, and she had laid up all the trays for the men's breakfast. That stupid paint stain she had made annoyed her again. She gave it a bit more scouring powder, but nothing seemed to work.

'Mother.'

'Mother? Since when . . .?'

Since Evie had called her mother that. Rose got up from her knees. 'I don't think you should put customers into that front room just now,' she said tensely.

'Why on earth not?'

'Well, er – it's still damp. They might – they might catch something.'

'Oh Rose, do stop being so *difficult*. Do you still believe this house is haunted?'

Rose was longing to say, 'Yes, I know it is,' but she knew she could not explain. She had to say, 'Who knows? Who cares?' and shut her mouth, like the shrugging, slapdash

114

adolescent she was supposed to be. This was her secret. A messenger of the grey horse must never tell. That was the hardest part, when her mind was a turmoil of emotions and fears and uncertainty about what came next. She could only tell Mr Vingo, and he had left her. He had told her what her job was, and then abandoned her.

'I wish I was a child again,' she told Ben.

'You still are.' He looked sideways down at her and laughed. He had asked her to run with him this morning (hooray), because it was his last day (hell).

'I'm not.' They were only jogging along the beach, so she was able to talk. 'But there are things about growing up that I'm not sure I like.'

'It gets better with the years,' Ben said, as if he were thirty-five. 'Come on, let's swim. I won't be here again till the end of the summer.'

They ran into the water, and she dived through a cresting wave into the clean, invigorating, uncomplicated sea. With Ben, she felt two tons lighter, and life was fun again.

After Ben left, there was nothing to distract her from the anxieties and suspense of this strange new life that had turned her life upside down and inside out at thirteen. The only hope was to try to pretend she was normal old Rose, and do her work.

Make beds. Fold towels. Slice string beans. Be nice to guests. Even to the Catchpole family, who talked and guffawed with their mouths full and called Rose 'Rosie' and behaved as if they owned the hotel. Lay tables. Wait at tables. Clear tables. A feeble job, compared to her glorious destiny as a messenger of the grey horse. But she did it as well as she could, and only spilled and dropped a few more things than usual.

'There she goes!' Two plates on the pantry floor, and a table full of Catchpoles greeting it like a chorus.

'Why do they yell out, "There she goes?"' Martin and Leonora were here for lunch, and he turned his wheelchair slightly so that he could frown at the Catchpoles, but they were eating pudding and didn't notice it.

'Because I'm clumsy.' Rose blushed.

'Don't you mind?'

'It's only a joke.' She could feel herself still blushing, because she did mind, and he knew it.

Rose thought that if she were tied to a wheelchair for the rest of her life, she would be crabby and self-centred. But Martin was always nice to everybody and seemed to take more interest in other people than himself.

After lunch, Martin got his chair out through the back door with the low doorstep, and he sat in the sun while Leonora, who had eaten too much steak and kidney pie, did some ballet exercises on the lawn. She was wearing a light skirt that flew out round her beautiful long pale legs. Her bare arms made graceful arcs and soft, enticing, flowing movements.

'I wish I had her shape.' Dilys looked out of the kitchen window. 'I marvel that she gave up her career as a dancer to look after him. Now me, I wouldn't do that for any man, because all you're going to get in the end is L.E.F.T., left.' Dilys should know. Her heart had been over the moon and then smashed in pieces twice in the last two weeks.

Rose went out with their coffee. She asked Leonora, 'Was it hard, having to give up being a dancer?'

'Yes, it was hard to admit that I couldn't go on with it. But I'd known all along that I might have to slow down, because of my heart.'

'Your heart?' In Rose's present state of nerves and insecurity, she jumped into fear that Leonora would have a heart attack and die.

'It's nothing, as long as I'm careful. And I've got Martin to look after me.' She put her head against his leg as she sat

116

Leonora did ballet exercises . . .

on the grass, and Rose wondered if she had invented the heart because she didn't want him to feel guilty that she had given up her career for him.

Mollie came out of the hotel and asked Rose if she had heard their good news.

'I'm to have a week's treatment at the clinic,' Martin said. 'I don't want to stay there, I've had enough of hospitals, so we're going to stay here and go in every day.'

'Since we haven't got a lift, I'll put them in the downstairs room in the annexe,' Mollie said.

'No, you can't,' Rose burst out, without thinking.

'Why not?' Her mother frowned at her: *Don't start that again.*

'Well . . . the Americans will still be here.'

'No, they'll be gone.'

'Won't it be fun?' Leonora said. 'We'll love being here. I'll teach you to dance, if you like. What's the matter, Rose?'

'Nothing.' Rose stood up.

'Not if you don't want to. You'd be good, though.'

Rose usually warmed to the smiling compliments that Leonora dished out, but she had turned back to go into the hotel, pleading to whatever gods might care, begging Favour, wherever he was: 'Not them. Oh please. Not them. Don't let the annexe do anything to them.'

When Mr Vingo came back, he wasn't quite the same. Not so helpful. He came whistling down the road one day, carrying that misshapen bag and swinging his stick in circles. Rose saw him from a window, and ran down to catch him before he came into the hotel.

'More strange things have happened,' she said urgently.

He raised his eyebrows. 'Hilda didn't overcook the beef? Someone didn't say, "Looks like rain again"?'

'Don't be silly. I mean . . .' She looked up at the people

118

sitting on the verandah. One of them was the thin American woman, draped in a plaid rug. She had been ill for two days.

'*The horse*,' Rose whispered.

'Been for a ride on old Moonlight, have you? That's good. Getting some rest from your labours.'

'No, *listen!*' Rose stamped her foot at him, but he went on up the front steps and into the hotel, with the bag bumping his knee, raising his stick in a jolly salute to the guests on the verandah.

She wasn't going to let him get away with this. She tackled him after lunch. Before he went upstairs, she went ahead of him and opened the door of the big linen cupboard and waited behind it to confront him on the way to his room.

'I think I've got the clue,' she whispered. 'I know what's wrong.'

'With what?'

'*You* know. The annexe house. I believe a man – it's horrible, but I believe a man killed himself there once. See, first I found out about it bringing out the worst in people. I thought that was it, but then I had to go back and see why. Then I found out there really was something wrong with the cupboard. It wasn't just me.'

He leaned on his stick patiently, blinking at her.

'And *then* I found out – I can't tell you now, but I'll tell you all about it some time, it was totally shattering – I found out exactly what it *was* about the cupboard.'

'Did you indeed?'

'It wasn't just Michael's shell-shock nightmare. It was true.' Everything was becoming clear, except Mr Vingo. He was still evasive, as if he were not really there. 'So that's what I had to find out,' she said flatly, her energy running out, because he was putting nothing into the conversation. 'Now what am I supposed to do?'

'Find out more, perhaps?' he enquired mildly. 'Excuse me, I have to go and say hello to my piano.'

'Rose.' Her father came through the door at the far end of the corridor that led to their own apartment. 'What are you doing?'

'Putting away towels.'

'I need your help.'

Mr Vingo had disappeared round the corner to his own little staircase, but as Rose turned to go with her father, she thought she heard him say, 'Courage, Rose.'

Philip Wood had plugged in a new type of electric pencil sharpener, which would sharpen different sized hard pencils and soft crayons at the same time, as long as you put them in the right slots, and he wanted to see if it was too difficult for a child. His work never seemed to be to find out what was good about new products, only what was bad about them, which did not improve his naturally gloomy view of life.

After they had wasted time going through, 'I'm not a child . . .' 'Well, pretend you are, for heaven's sake. Just this once, do something for me without arguing . . .' etc. etc., Rose disappointed him by finding the right slots. As the motor whirred and spun, eating up the pencils and crayons, there spun through it the sound of Mr Vingo's piano, which Rose had never heard from this room, playing the tune of the hidden valley.

She went to the door.

'Just one more thing, Rose.'

'Can it wait?' She opened the door.

'Oh well,' he said resignedly. 'I suppose so. Oh yes. Everything can always wait till someone else has got time.'

Rose's bicycle was leaning against the garage. She rode through the wood, leaned the bike against a tree and headed out towards the moor.

The rock was there. The secret path through the trees and thick undergrowth was there. The valley was there – it must be, although its edge was obscured by the swirling mist. Rose put out a foot, feeling for ground that wasn't there. It took tremendous courage to go down into that pit of unknown demons. If only there were some other way to reach the bridge and cross it on to Favour's sunlit slope. Why did he put his messengers through this terrible ordeal? To prove he could protect them, or to test whether they had the fire and spirit to do his work? What happened if they failed?

I'm not brave enough to go down there. Rose stepped back towards the safety of the trees, and at once the insistent tune in her head became the thunder of hoofs and the ringing scream of a horse enraged and fighting.

'Forward!' the ringing noise called to her. 'Come to me – hurry!' And she knew she was more afraid of Favour's wrath than of the voices and ghouls that she must struggle through to reach him.

She shut her eyes and plunged down into the mist. The guttural voices and the laughter were somewhere around her, but they kept away. She stumbled against a stone and opened her eyes, full into the crafty, darting eyes of a man no taller than her. Spindly and crooked, he wore a black robe trimmed with spiky black fur, and on his shoulder, nestled against his yellow sneering cheek and wiry hair, a tiny brown weasel with huge protruding eyes crouched with bared teeth and hissed at her like a snake.

The Lord of the Moor!

Rose screamed and flung out her arms, but there was nothing there to hit. She ran right through him into the bright air and the gleam of the swift-running river. Favour did not appear until she was across the bridge and half way up the other side, and then he suddenly charged out right above her in a blaze of light that shook sparks off his mane as he tossed his head – *hurry, hurry* – and flicked his ears back and forth, and trampled to be off.

Hurry, hurry. He carried her away, and they were part of

the rushing wind. *Hurry, hurry*. The wind roared in her ears, and 'Hurry!' a voice echoed, and a small bell rang, tinkle, tinkle. 'Hurry up, girl, for the dear Lord's sake do, or they'll have our livers.'

She picked up the heavy silver dish of meat and potatoes and carried it across the hall and into the dining-room.

'What took you so long, Winnie?' a woman with a handsome, disgruntled face asked sharply. She was sitting at the table with a man and three children.

'Dunno, mum.' Winnie was very young to be a maid, so it must be ages ago, before child labour laws. She was wearing a black dress with a cap of some kind, and an apron with frills on it. She handed round the food. The dish was heavy and hot. The children fussed and picked as they helped themselves, and kept her standing, taking the heat and weight of the dish first on the flat of one hand, then the other. Even the little boy, who looked about three, was allowed to take too many potatoes, and mess the meat and gravy about.

His mother had leaned over to correct him, but the father said, 'Don't hold him back, Catherine. Let him be a man.'

There was a boy of about ten and a girl of about seven or eight. The girl said impudently to her mother, 'When are you going out to buy another baby? Billie isn't any fun to play with any more.'

'Oh, spare us,' the older boy said. 'Not another *baby*.'

'Hush, children. It's not your business. If I want to buy another baby, I will. If not, I won't.'

'*We* won't,' the father said. 'There's enough trouble in this world already, without bringing another child into it.'

'Children don't bring the trouble,' the girl said demurely. 'The grown-ups do that.'

'That's enough, Alice,' the mother snapped, and the father said, 'Let the child talk.' It seemed that they had to contradict each other.

In the kitchen with the cook, there was another woman called Margery who was a maid and a nurse, but she was grumpy and crossed in love, which was why Winnie had to do most of the waiting in the dining-room today. 'Give you some practice, girl.' The family called her Winnie. The other maids called her 'girl'.

'I don't like being in the dining-room. I don't like what they say to each other.'

'Don't criticize your betters,' Cook said, but she added, 'I don't blame you. If that's marriage, Margery, you may be better off without it.'

'Those children are paying for it.' Margery pouted. 'When there's trouble brewing, they play up. They'll get spoiled.'

The little boy had been allowed to get down from the table without finishing his potatoes and climb on his father's knee, where the father caressed him, not smiling, but as a man might caress a small dog, with a yearning fondness.

'Billie is spoiled,' Cook declared, 'but he's the Master's treasure. His pride and joy. His only joy, you might say. He's like a week of wet Sundays.'

'I think there's money worries.' Margery dropped her voice and talked behind her hand. 'Now, girl, you shut your ears.'

'Gambling?' Cook narrowed her eyes.

'You never know. But he's been so gloomy lately, and one day when he come home out of spirits, I heard the Mistress ask him for money for something, and he asked her if she thought she could get blood out of a stone.'

Cook and Margery went off to put their feet up, leaving Winnie to wash up and sweep the kitchen. The water that came out of the stiff brass tap was brownish and not very hot. Her hands were chapped from the winter, and it made her back ache, leaning over the low sink. As she toiled away, using a bar of yellow soap to try to get the grease off the plates, she was so tired and homesick that she cried a little. The tears that dropped into the sink were hotter than the scummy water. After she dried her sore hands, she put them under her arms to try to warm them before she got out the broom.

There was a braided rag rug where the meal trolley had stood when this house was a hospital. She picked up the rug to sweep under it, and saw a dark stain on the wood floor. She got the yellow soap and went down on her knees to scrub it. No use, so she put the rug back down over it before Cook could see.

Winnie slept in a sort of cupboard off the kitchen, where there was room for just a bed and some hooks for her clothes. She did not take off anything except her shoes, because it was cold.

She was up early, sweeping, dusting, bringing in coal. Outside in the frosty morning, Rose saw that the fruit trees were young and newly planted. The agent who sold the house to Mollie Wood had said that the apple trees were about eighty years old. There were little fences round the new trees, because two ponies with winter coats were in the orchard, a good looking bay and an old white cob with a short tail. Next door, where her own house ought to be, a large cellar hole, and piles of planks and bricks and slates showed that it was going to be built.

Winnie knelt to clean out the grates in the downstairs rooms and lay fires. Brushing the stairs, also on hands and knees, which was where a lot of her time was spent, she heard voices from behind a bedroom door.

'Where are you, Catherine?' the Master said sadly. 'I can't reach you any more.'

His wife gave him an abrupt answer in her sharp, impatient voice.

'I had such a bad night,' he said. 'I dreamed I was caught in a dark pit. I stretched up my hand, but I couldn't reach yours.'

124

Winnie heard the Mistress say something sarcastic about too many glasses of port. 'You're not the only one whose night was disturbed,' she said. 'I woke and heard someone crying. I got up to look at the children, but they were asleep.'

When Winnie, in a print dress and apron, went in with a brass jug of hot water and drew the curtains, the Mistress asked her, 'You don't cry in the night, Winnie, do you?'

'No, mum.'

'You're such a quiet girl. You see everything and say nothing.'

'Yes, mum.'

Later, Winnie was called up to the bedroom to help the dressmaker, who came for a fitting. The dress was an ugly green, which did not soften the Mistress's hard good looks. Winnie was on her knees again, measuring the hem three inches from the floor and putting in pins, while the dressmaker fussed about with tucks and seams above her.

'So you really do like this house, madam.' The dressmaker was a sharp-faced, gossipy woman, hissing through a row of pins she held in her mouth. 'Well, I'm glad to hear that, I must say, under the circumstances. They say houses have an atmosphere, don't they, but I'm glad to know that isn't the case with your beautiful home.'

'Why should it have an atmosphere?' The Mistress moved impatiently, and Winnie had to reset some of the pins.

'They didn't tell you anything? Oh well then, it's all for the best, isn't it, and no doubt you'll be hearing some local stories as you get to know people in the neighbourhood.'

'I doubt that. So far, I haven't met anyone I'd take the trouble to know,' the Mistress said. 'And please don't start talking foolish nonsense to my husband if you see him downstairs. He's gloomy enough as it is. Nothing is right these days.'

'He looks jolly enough now, madam.'

They were standing near the window. Finishing the hem and getting up, Winnie saw the Master with Billie on the drive outside the stable. He was harnessing the bay pony to a two-wheeled dog-cart.

His wife flung open the window and called down. 'Be careful, James! That pony's not to be trusted.'

'He's all right,' the father called back. 'Billie loves him. We're going to drive down to the village.'

'Take Snowball then.'

'He's lame.'

'It's too cold for Billie.'

'He's bundled up.'

'The roads may be icy. Oh – he's too tiresome for words.' She shut the window with a bang. 'Winnie, run down and bring Master Billie inside this instant.'

When Winnie went outside, Billie, wrapped in a coat and a huge red muffler, was already on the high seat of the cart with his father, squirming with excitement, his eyes bright.

'Excuse me, sir, the Mistress says Master Billie is to come indoors.'

Billie set up a wail, and his father looked down at Winnie and said coldly. 'You won't understand this, but she doesn't want the children to like me.'

Winnie stepped quickly back as he laid the whip across the pony's back and drove off round the side of the house. As Rose listened to them clattering away down the frosty road, she wanted to go away too. A sense of foreboding filled her. She wanted to get out of this. Perhaps if she slept, she might sleep her way out of it, as before. God knows, she was tired enough. She would lie down and sleep and wake up on the moor.

She dodged Cook and went to her room. She slept, and woke thinking she was in her own room at home. Where was the window? Why was it so dark? There was no light switch by the bed. She sat up, and her long greasy hair straggled over her face. She was still Winnie.

The kitchen was empty. She opened the back door to see if the bay pony had come back, and saw the dejected old white horse looking at her, with his head down. As she returned his stare, all at once his head went up, and he grew and quivered and was splendid and graceful with his flowing tail and his shining dark grey eyes, staring and staring.

'Take me away!' ,she called to him. She did not know if she actually spoke the words, nor whether it was his word or his thought that gave her back the answer.

'Not yet.'

'Shut that door, girl. Do you want to freeze us all to death?'

'No, Cook.'

'And go and see who that is at the door. Margery is out with Tom and Alice.'

A man was at the door in a leather coat and heavy boots. Beyond him in the road stood a tradesman's van with two horses. The man said nothing, but looked beyond Winnie to where the children's mother was coming into the hall from the sitting-room.

'What is it?'

The man did not speak. Behind him, the father climbed out of the van and walked slowly towards the house, carrying across his arms the bundled-up child, with the long red scarf trailing.

The mother blamed the father, and he bowed his head and accepted the guilt. She had told him the pony was not safe. She had told him not to take Billie. The pony had shied, and Billie was thrown out on to the road.

'You killed him.' She kept on and on, hysterically. In the kitchen they did not know how the poor man could stand it.

The mother's sister came, and they stayed upstairs,

The father walked slowly . . .

weeping in the little boy's room. The grandmother came and took the older children away. When the father went upstairs to sit beside the dead child, his wife would not let him go into the room.

He sat in the cold dining-room. When Winnie was sent tiptoeing in to see if he wanted anything to eat, she found him in his black mourning suit and black cravat, sitting at the table with his arms limply out before him. At his side, turned towards him, was Billie's chair with the thick cushion. That night, when Winnie tried to sleep, and Rose fought to help her sleep, so that she could escape, she heard the man pacing, up and down the stairs, in and out of the dining-room, back and forth in the hall, pacing, pacing.

The men in black came in the morning. The mother would not come down to see them take the child away. Margery was with her, so Cook sent Winnie to find the Master. He was not at the table in the dining-room. The door of the china cupboard stood open. As Winnie went to shut it, she had to look into the cupboard. In the space round the back corner, the man in his black clothes was hanging by a rope from a hook.

She ran screaming through the house, ran into someone, clutched them, and fainted.

Rose woke with difficulty on the moor, as if she were climbing up out of a pit. Her legs felt like lead. Her arms were wrapped tightly round herself. After she stood up, for quite a long time, they ached from her rigid clutching.

CHAPTER ELEVEN

It was not surprising that one of the Americans was ill. 'A virus,' she called it, but Rose knew better. She was sick herself, sick with longing for the days when nothing much happened, and she was an ordinary child who had never known sorrow or fear. When her father said he was going on an overnight trip, she surprised him by asking if she could come too.

She avoided Mr Vingo. She wanted to tell him about her last ghastly journey into the past, but she did not want to run the risk of hearing the tune, or of being summoned by the horse, ever again. Let him find another messenger. The only thing she did for Favour – well, it was for herself really – was to go to the annexe kitchen and look again at the impenetrable stain on the new floor tile. It was under the table, under the window, where Winnie had put the rug back down over the stain she could not scrub out of the wood floor.

So. She had found another clue, for what that was worth. There was nothing she could do about it now. The stain had been made years and years ago, and had somehow been able to penetrate through from under the tile. She had also confirmed what she already knew: that the house had a bad effect on people. Even the dressmaker had hinted at it, and the Master had been so unhappy even before the child was killed. Was the child fated to be killed, because of the house? Was that what it could do to people? Had Michael died in the end, or Mr Carter upstairs with the terrible wound? Would that nice American woman die of pneumonia if she didn't get out of that room she called her safe haven?

She recovered. She and her friend got into their car and

drove away towards Scotland. Rose and her father left right after them, and Rose was glad to get away. She would try to be nicer to him, like when they used to go on trips when she was an innocent child, more willing to listen to his lectures and to laugh at his jokes, which you were never sure were jokes.

Mollie wanted them to take her car, but he refused.

'The Master wants to drive *his* car.' Rose said. She had decided to call him that.

They started noisily off in his old car to drive the two hundred miles to the food factory where he was to discuss his report on tinned soups and frozen meat pies. The car rattled and was draughty and uncomfortable, but it reminded Rose of days gone by when she was too small to see through the windscreen unless she sat on a cushion, so she was content.

She slept during the journey.

'You need to go away for a holiday,' her father said.

'I live in a holiday place.'

'Other people are having holidays there. You're working.'

'I often think I'm having a better time than they are. I have enough time off to ride, or go to the beach. I like work.' She looked at her bare arm and flexed it to see how the biceps muscle was developing.

'You're just like your mother.'

'Good.'

They had quite a nice time. He was better company on the road. They stayed in a hotel that was not nearly as nice as Wood Briar, and had a rotten dinner there with a man from the factory. He and Rose's father discussed the pros and cons of 1,000 milligrams of sodium per chicken pie, and the relative risks of monosodium glutamate versus disodium guanylate as flavour enhancers for soup. It was humdrum and safe.

Over the coffee, the man from the factory said earnestly, 'Now, I suppose we'll have to talk about sensory merits and defects.'

'What's that?' Rose asked.

'Smell and taste.'

'I'd have thought you'd want to know about that first,' Rose said. 'I mean, whatever is in the soup, people aren't going to buy it if they don't like the taste.'

'Good point.' The man nodded seriously. 'Have you ever tried any of our soups?'

'We mostly make our own at the hotel, but we use your tomato sometimes on Sunday nights.'

Her father tutted. 'It contains 2.5 grams of sugar per serving.'

'You and Mr Lancaster have drunk three glasses of wine.' Rose had had half a glass herself, with soda. 'That's got far more sugar than a little innocent cream of tomato soup.'

'Good for you, Rose,' Mr Lancaster said admiringly. 'Bright kid you've got there, Philip. She's quite special.'

'Don't let that put you off,' Philip Wood said, to hide the fact that he was pleased. 'She's very ordinary really, aren't you, my Rose?'

Oh, my Daddy, if you only knew . . .

While he was at the factory meeting next day, Rose walked down to the town park to sit on a bench in the sun and read, and enjoy the feeling of having nothing to do.

On the artificial lake, children were throwing bread for the ducks, and two small boys prodded with sticks at a toy sailboat, trying to make it cross the water against the breeze. Old ladies dragged small dogs away from the smells they wanted to smell. A skinny old man in trousers belted with string did his rounds of the waste baskets. Mothers pushed babies about. One woman had twins in a tandem pushchair, face to face, bashing at each other while she talked with a friend.

A lumpish, awkward young man with thick eyebrows and a ragged moustache walked aimlessly past Rose. He went round and round the small park. He wore grubby jeans and a torn T-shirt and had a rather lost air of having nothing to do and nowhere to go. The fourth or fifth time he passed her, he stopped and came back to her bench, lifting his soft moustache in a smile, half eager, half uncertain.

'Nice day.'

She looked up, then went on reading.

'I said, "Nice day."' The eyebrows growing close together at the top of his nose would have looked fierce, if the rest of his face had been stronger. 'Please will you look up?'

'Why?'

'I want to see if I was right.'

'I'm not somebody you know, if that's what you mean.' She looked up.

He gazed at her rather sadly. 'I think you are.'

'I don't know you.' And I don't want to know you now, she thought. She needed to be alone, resting with her book, away from the complications of home.

He was muttering to himself as he sat down on the bench, too close to her. 'Beauty and strength,' he whispered. 'Grace without vi'lence . . .'

'What's that?'

'*You* know.'

Safer not to answer.

'How long you been hearing the tune?'

'Go away.'

'Look,' he said, 'don't put me on. I know who you are, see?'

'Who am I, then?'

'One of us.'

Oh God. She knew there had been other messengers, but she wasn't prepared to meet one.

133

'The tune,' he said. 'How long have you – *you* know?'
She shifted away from him.

'With me, it was at about your age. Crazy about horses I
was, for some reason, though I'd never been nearer to one
than a police horse I once patted in London, or going to the
races with Dad. We was living in Newcome then, before
Dad left. When I found the grey horse, see, it was like
finding a whole new world that had been waiting for me and
where I really counted for something. Since I lost all that,
nothing's gone right. Said goodbye to a couple of jobs
through daydreaming, but when you've got that beautiful
wise white spirit to dream about . . .'

He turned to her with a pathetic, pleading look of failure
that Rose could not bear. She shut her book and stood up. 'I
don't know what you're talking about.'

As she turned to walk away, she was knocked over by a
mighty rush of wind, and a thunder of hoofs galloped over
her, with the beat of her crime: deny, deny, deny.

She was lying on the ground because her ankle had turned
on the rough ground, and she had tripped over her long
skirt.

'Where are you?' A woman's voice. 'Where are you,
Lilian?'

'Out here, Aunt Beth.' Lilian sat up and rubbed her
ankle. 'I came out to see where you're going to plant the
orchard, and my silly ankle turned.'

'Oh dear, not again.' Lilian's Aunt Beth was standing in
the back doorway of a brand new brick house. There was no
ivy, but Rose knew it was the annexe as it had originally
been, about a hundred years ago, when the house was built.
'Get up off the damp grass and come indoors. Your mother
will be angry with me if I let you catch cold.'

'Yes, they've got to take care of me,' Lilian thought
smugly. 'Because I am delicate.'

She got up and brushed herself off with a hand in a scratchy lace mitten. She wore a long green dress with a lot of unnecessary frills and ornaments. It was bunched up behind over many flounced petticoats, which made it difficult to move freely. On her head was a bonnet, tied with wide ribbons under the chin. From within Lilian's bonnet, Rose looked out to see not only no garden or sheds behind the brand new house, but no larger house next door. Where the Wood Briar Hotel was to be her home a hundred years later, there was just a large field with buttercups and black and white cows in it.

'Come along, dear. We'll have some refreshment. I want to show you the new fabric for the settee.'

They went through into the front room. Lilian's Aunt Beth wore an apricot dress, the same colour as her piled-up hair, the skirt rising into a high bustle at the back, with ruffles round it. With her bosom pushed up and also ruffled, and her bottom sticking out, she looked like a strutting pigeon. She was beautiful and graceful and kind, and Rose was praying that nothing terrible was going to happen to her. She had a strong feeling that this scene she had travelled into was going to be crucial, and that some final clue would be found here that would explain the lasting unhappiness in the house.

The front room was quite elaborate, with plump new furniture, a gilt framed mirror over the marble mantelpiece, a wealth of ornaments, long brocade curtains. Beth seemed very happy here, and talked as if she loved and admired her husband Ronald, who was away on business for a few days, which was why Lilian was here, to keep Beth company.

Poor company, Rose thought. Lilian was rather silly and nervous. She felt strange in the new house, because she had liked Beth and Ronald's old poky house in the village, in which she had spent many happy childhood days. She did not want to be grown up. She hung her head and blushed when spoken to, and was frightened of Beth's little pug dog, and would not drink a small glass of sweet madeira wine with the shortcake.

When Beth took her out for a walk on the sandy path through the dunes across the road to where they could look out over the sea, Lilian kept stumbling in her little button boots, and asking when they could turn back, and squealing every time the pug raced back to them, and flapping her hands at the seagulls.

'Once,' she told Beth, 'we were on deck on the Channel steamer, and an enormous savage gull swooped down and snatched a cake out of my hand.'

Beth laughed. 'What did you do?'

'I fainted,' Lilian said proudly.

'Well, don't faint now. Just come through this gap, and then we can see the beautiful shining sea. Isn't it the grandest, loveliest sight in the world? Oh, I'm so glad I live here, Lily! Smell that wonderful air.'

Lilian sniffed delicately. Beth threw back her head, and the sea wind pulled her apricot hair from under her hat and blew it round her radiant face. 'Look at those fishing boats out there, making for the harbour. One of them must be Joe's. He's the fisherman I told you about. I see him sometimes when I go to visit his sick mother in the village. He's –' She giggled and bent her head to confide in Lilian. 'Well, he's a little sweet on me, you know. He came to see me yesterday after Ronald left, but of course I had to tell him that wouldn't do.'

'Oh, that's romantic,' Lilian said soppily, putting her head and bonnet on one side and staring dreamily at the sea, which she didn't much care for.

'Hush, Lilian. It could never be. I love my husband, and he's a very jealous man. If he ever knew anything about Joe . . . Oh goodness, that reminds me. Joe left his jacket behind when he came to the house, and I put it in the parlour cupboard. I must get it back to him before Ronald comes home.'

'Won't you keep it for a sentimental keepsake, Aunt Beth?'

'Oh no, child. You don't understand anything about marriage. You don't know what you're saying.'

'*You can say that again,*' Rose thought. Lilian did not know much about anything. It was a curious experience to inhabit such an empty head.

'Perhaps tomorrow you could take it down to his mother's cottage for me,' Beth suggested.

'I'll be too tired. Let's go back,' said whiny Lilian. 'My ankle hurts.'

They were in the parlour playing cards when there was a clatter of hoofs on the road outside, and they looked out of the window to see Beth's husband Ronald jump out of the station cab. He ran up the path, and when they heard the front door bang shut, Beth moved instinctively to the cupboard and stood against the door.

When Ronald came in, his eyes were wild and his hair disordered. He did not look at Lilian, or speak to her. He shut the door and said angrily to Beth, 'Well, it didn't take much time, did it?'

'What do you mean? Why are you back so soon? I mean, I'm glad to see you, but I hadn't expected you back for two days.'

'Of course not. So it didn't take long to invite that – that – for God's sake, Beth – a common fisherman!'

'I didn't invite him. He came with a message from his mother. Don't get in such a state. Look, you're upsetting poor Lily. Calm down, dear.' Beth tried to soothe him, but Ronald was blazing with rage.

'That's not what I heard. Oh yes, I wasn't long in Newcome before a busybody gossip sought me out to tell me what all the world knew – except me, the betrayed husband. How long has this been going on? How long was he here yesterday?'

'He didn't come in. He just – he just came to the door.' Although she had nothing to hide, Beth began to stammer and lie from fear. Under a chair, the pug growled. Lilian stood by the window transfixed, looking from one to the other, and wishing she could faint.

'In our own house!'

'Don't spoil it, Ronald. I love this house. I want it to stay happy.'

'Happy? This house will never be happy again.'

'Ronald!' she cried in horror.

'Come here. Come here and tell me the truth.'

He looked so threatening that Beth still stood by the cupboard door, unable to move. Ronald strode across the room, knocking down the card table. 'What are you hiding there?' The pug growled again and leaped at his leg as he pushed Beth roughly away from the cupboard and flung open the door. He picked up a heavy dark blue jacket and threw it disgustedly on to the new flowered carpet. It brought a damp smell of the sea into the stuffy, overcrowded room.

'So he never came into the house!'

'Don't, don't – if he did, I told him to go.' Beth was crying. 'Help me, Lilian. You know what's true . . . Ronald, please believe me. Oh, why can't I reach you? I love you, only you. Lily, tell him – help me!'

'Don't drag the child into this.' Ronald was standing dangerously still, staring at Beth with cold eyes, full of pain and hatred. 'Leave the room, Lilian.'

'No, stay,' Beth begged, but although Rose struggled to put some guts into her, cowardly Lilian was glad to escape from the room.

In the hall, she tried to make herself faint, a talent she had cultivated, to get attention. She cast herself on to the sofa, moaning weakly.

Get back in there and help Beth, you fool, Rose urged, but Lilian only cried feebly for help, and held her breath to make herself dizzy.

Rose woke with Lilian's feeble moans fading in her ears. She was lying on the grass of the little park with the sun on her face. The young man with the moustache was gone. The woman with the tandem twins was still talking to her friend, whose child leaned steeply sideways at the end of her arm, trying to pull her away.

Rose went back to the hotel. She packed her bag and waited in the hall for her father.

'Don't you want lunch?' he asked.

'Let's get a sandwich on the road. I want to get back.'

'Don't bother asking me how the meeting went,' he said when they were in the car.

'Oh. Sorry.' Rose was brooding.

'Because I'll tell you anyway. Triumph of P. Wood. They couldn't argue their case. Their chemists were bluffing. They take the minestrone off the market within six months, and the turkey pie will go too, unless they sharpen up that soggy wet crust.'

Rose was too distracted to tell him that she rather liked the sodden pastry soaked with gravy at the bottom of a pie.

At home, she told her mother, 'The Master and I had a smashing time.'

'No fights?'

'No.'

'Honestly?'

'When I lie, you don't believe me. When I tell the truth, you don't believe me either.' From the kitchen window, Rose saw Mr Vingo at the laundry line, hanging out a pair of swimming trunks shaped like a bucket, and went outside to talk to him.

They went to the triangular side verandah, which was

usually empty after the early morning sun had left it. Rose climbed up over the rail, and tried to help him over, but he got stuck with one leg half over, and she thought he was going to have a heart attack, so she had to push him back down, and he went round into the hotel and came back to her through the glass door.

'Not now, Colin.' He was pursued through the door by a tiny boy in long shorts, who had taken to him because he carried toffees. Colin, who could barely talk, babbled something that ended in 'Stavingo?' Which was what he called Mr Vingo.

'Run along, there's a good chap.' But the child had climbed securely into one of the basket chairs, so he gave him a toffee and let him stay. 'Because he can't understand, and if he could, he can't talk about it.'

Breathlessly, Rose told him something about the latest journeys she had taken through time, and the extraordinary things she had discovered.

'You're listening to me now, Mr Vingo. Last time, you went all weird and distant. You wouldn't listen. I couldn't reach you.'

(Couldn't reach you . . . That was what the Master had said in the bedroom, and what Beth had said to Ronald. 'Why can't I reach you?')

'Sorry. Clumsy ass, I was, but I knew you had to do it by yourself. You thought you had all the clues, but you didn't, of course. You had to go back and find more. And you did, my trusty Rose of all roses.'

'O of aw oses,' from Colin.

'I had to,' Rose said. 'Look – with Favour, you don't choose. For a hero of peace, he can be dreadfully violent.'

'Don't forget he was a war horse once. He has to be strong. What power would he have, if he didn't make the sternest demands on his messengers?'

'That's another thing.' Rose frowned. 'I met this man –

140

well, boy really – who pretended he was one of us. He wasn't special in any way, except specially sort of a failure. He couldn't be a messenger.'

'Doesn't follow.' Mr Vingo leaned back in the wicker chair, and Colin came and climbed with difficulty into what would have been his lap if he had one, and started going through his pockets. 'I mean, look at Silly Hugh. He was no great shakes. Look at Leo of Pilot Rock, who used to save ships at sea from the phantom light that lured them on to the shoals. He was a hunchback, they say, with a purple lump on the side of his head. Not exactly prepossessing. Look at me, for that matter.'

She looked at him. 'But when you were thirteen . . .'

'I could have helped you then. Now you stand alone. You too, Colin. Get down, you're a crook.'

Colin tumbled off his lap, squeezed between two railings and fell on to the grass.

'Let's see,' Mr Vingo went on. 'Going backwards from the birthday party, what have we got? Something wrong with cupboard. What? House brings out worst in people. Why? Cupboard haunted by ghost of man hanging. Why? Because man did hang self. Why? Because house soured his marriage. Why? Because something dreadful happened there, connected with jacket in cupboard.'

'Ronald,' Rose said. 'What do you think he did to poor Beth? Why didn't he believe her? I'm so afraid of what happened. I could kill that creep Lilian for – my God, Stavingo, *do you suppose he killed her?* The stain. The stain that won't come out. *Blood.*' She had thought that many times.

'There's only one way to find out.'

'I've got to get back, haven't I?' Rose bit on a fingernail. 'I've got to find out the truth, and stop the annexe from destroying any more people with its history of unhappiness. But what could I do? What's done is done. It's too late.'

141

'Never too late to restore love. Don't you see – don't you *see* – that this is the horse's glorious mission for you?'

A thrill went through her, as if this were the beginning of the adventure, not the end.

'What will I do?'

'Who can say? You'll know when you get there. You have to go back.'

'Play the piano for me then, Stavingo. Help me to find the horse.'

'I can't play,' Mr Vingo said. 'I cut my finger.' He held up a fat bandage, making a child's face for sympathy. Rose wouldn't give him any. He had suddenly gone distant and unreachable again, and the bandage might be a fake.

She got Joyce to let her take Moonlight out alone again, and tried to find the path to the rock. She roamed the moor on foot, but without the tune she could not find the way to the valley. She went into the scullery while the dishwasher was running, and watched the television to see if someone would speak to her. She stood on the lawn on the place where the summer house had been, clenching her teeth and her fists.

'Patience.' Mr Vingo leaned out of the turret window, like Rapunzel. 'Wait.'

CHAPTER TWELVE

It was hard to give her mind to anything, when all the time her ears were half listening for the call of the grey horse. Sometimes she longed for it. Sometimes she dreaded it. What terrible violence might she have to see? Even if she knew what to do, how could she force Lilian to do it? What happened to messengers who failed?

Wait. Patience.

It was better when Martin and Leonora came back to stay. Rose spent as much time with them as she could, partly because she liked being with them, partly to keep watch for anything bad the annexe house might do to them.

Martin came in and out of the hotel through the back door, and Jim Fisher made a board ramp up the steps to the french window of the annexe lounge, so that Leonora could push his chair from the garden to the house.

Watching him come out, Rose saw him spin the outer wheels with his powerful arms and whizz down the ramp by himself, with Leonora running anxiously behind. When he stopped safely in the grass, Leonora turned a perfect cartwheel, to show she could still do it. Sometimes she practised, holding on to a fence rail and moving her legs and body in the *barre* exercises. Sometimes she danced for him in a lavender-coloured leotard, in and out of the apple trees, while he sat in his chair and watched her, his eyes absorbed, smiling his easy, relaxed smile. They were very much in love.

Rose was worried all the time about them being in the haunted room, for fear their happiness and trust in each other might be spoiled. And yet, could it be a good thing?

'To restore love,' Mr Vingo had said. Was it possible that by Martin and Leonora being in the house, their love might help to bring some peace to all the sadness and cruelties of a hundred years?

Leonora thought Rose was very good-looking. She was the first person who had ever said that, except Mollie, and mothers didn't count because they said that anyway.

She insisted on giving Rose a white sun dress with a low square neck and full skirt. When Rose tried it on after the hem was shortened, Leonora brought her Polaroid camera out to the garden to take a picture. Rose sat on the tree stump by Martin's chair, with the dress spread out round her.

As the picture began to develop, you could see a very large white blur at the side of the wheelchair.

'I over-exposed it,' Leonora said, but Rose caught her breath and took the picture and turned away with it, because she could see that the developing image was the grey horse, lying proudly but calmly on the grass by the wheelchair, with his tail fanned out behind him.

If only Martin could step on to Favour's back and ride! Then this image was gone as the picture developed more clearly, and there was only Rose, scowling self-consciously in her unfamiliar white dress.

But she had seen. The message was clear. *So it's now,* she said silently to Favour. *All right. I'm ready.*

Rose got up. 'Going to work?' Leonora asked. She was never one of the people who said, 'You're doing too much,' or, 'Don't work too hard.' Dancers knew about hard work, day after day, and taking care of Martin must be just as hard, day after day.

'Actually, I've got the afternoon off. I thought I'd go up on the moor for a bit.' Rose shifted from foot to foot, keyed up, anxious to be off now that the time was here.

'We'll come with you.' Martin was leaning back with his face to the sun, eyes closed, smiling. He always looked more peaceful and amiable than most people who have no pain and the use of all their limbs.

'I think I'll stay here,' Leonora said. 'I'm a bit tired.'

His eyes opened at once and his face was serious. 'Are you all right?'

'Of course. Don't be silly. I just feel I should stay here. You go with Rose, if she'll take you.'

'I'd love that.' Martin looked genuinely pleased, so Rose couldn't say no, although she was aching to go to the valley. But perhaps she could go there with Martin. Ben had not been able to see it, but perhaps because the horse lay by his chair for a moment, it meant that Martin could. 'Where shall we go, Rose?'

'Wherever we want.'

They went through the hotel garden to the wood. By pushing the outer wheels with his strong arms, Martin could move the wheelchair over level ground as fast as Rose could walk. Some of the way, she had to push him, over tree roots and round muddy patches. When they got to the slope beyond the wood, she knew she could never get him up there through the long grass and the bushes, and there was no gate in the wall beyond. They turned along the gravel lane to go round through the farmyard and up the cart track, to the moor on the other side of the walled pasture. There was no one about in the farmyard, except a chained dog who barked at the wheelchair.

Out on the moor, Martin noticed everything, a lark high up, the shapes of clouds, the different colours of the long grass when the wind ran through it, the way two poplars by a stream turned their leaves inside out, silver to green, green to silver, the horseshoe marks of hoofs on the turf.

He stopped. 'Is this where you ride?'

'Sometimes.'

'Think of me when you do. God!' He threw back his head and for a moment his amiable face was clenched as if in pain. 'If I could ever be on a horse again, I'd die happy.'

If only she could take him with her on Favour. She almost began to tell him what it was like to ride into the wind on the powerful grey horse, but suddenly she heard the beckoning notes of the tune, calling her to hurry.

'Are you tired?' she asked Martin.

'A bit. Let's stop here and enjoy the sun and the view.'

'I need to run. You stay here and I'll be right back.'

As she ran ahead, she looked back once and saw that he was not looking at the far off hills, but down at the ground where the hoof tracks were.

When she came to the giant rock and pushed through the undergrowth of the trees to the valley, Rose was no longer afraid. She felt strong. She dropped confidently down through the mist. The demon shapes receded, and she was quickly out into the light and across the bridge and scrambling fast up to the horse, and swiftly on to his back and away.

The wind shrieked past her, and its voice became a woman's voice, screaming, crying hysterically.

Lilian and Rose were in the kitchen doorway, trembling with fear. Lilian wanted to turn and run upstairs and bury her head under the bedclothes, but Rose grabbed her from within and made her stay.

Beth had run into the kitchen, holding the fisherman's jacket, and Ronald had followed her, still blazing with fury.

'But it's lies,' Beth kept sobbing, 'all lies. There's no one but you – I swear – Oh, why can't I make you see? I'm so stupid . . .' The same words Rose had used, and had heard Felicity use when she burned the toast, in the same spot. 'You must believe me!'

He would not listen, and Beth could hardly speak. She

was half collapsed against the sink, weeping with jagged, rending sobs. The pug went towards her, and her husband kicked it away savagely back across the room. He was like a madman. Against he told Lilian to get out. Again Rose forced her to stay, and with a giant effort of will she made Lilian step forward in the green dress puffed out with petticoats.

'Have mercy, Uncle!' she begged in her high, childish voice.

'Get away from me. Get back!' he raged at poor terrified Lilian, striking her roughly on the arm and knocking her away. She could only watch in horror as he snatched up a kitchen knife and stabbed threateningly at the jacket. Weeping hysterically, Beth tried to get to the back door, but he was there before her. She was trapped against the wall under the window, cringing, pleading with him.

She was standing in the very place where Rose knew the stain was on the floor, the blood persisting for a hundred years. Oh God – don't let it happen! He lunged again at the jacket. Beth tried to snatch it away, the knife went into her breast, and she fell backward by the window.

'I've killed her!' Ronald gave a crazed, unearthly scream and rushed outside.

Dying, Beth cried to Lilian, 'Help me!' but Lilian had fallen to the floor in a faint. 'Help me!' Through the dizzying blackness in which she had fallen, Rose clearly heard Leonora's voice. Beth's agonized cries were Leonora's. 'Help me! Help me!'

A rush of wind swept over Rose, and with the wind, in a thunder of hoofs, came the great horse Favour.

'Help me!' Leonora's voice was fainter.

'I'm coming!' Rose cried. The white glow of the horse's energy was all about her. She was caught up somehow, and then she was on his back. The strong arch of his neck rose in

147

Beth was trapped against the wall . . .

front of her. His mane streamed back in her face. She shouted again, and they galloped out into the sky. Beyond the sunset, beyond the flaming streaks of clouds gathering in to the western edge of the world, they flew through roaring space, hurtling forward through time until Rose woke on the grass at the back of the annexe house with Leonora's voice still in her ears.

She picked herself up, shaking her head to clear it, and rushed into the kitchen. Leonora had collapsed half under the table, her hand over her heart. Her colour was ghastly. She was sweating and trembling. She managed a faint smile at Rose, which became a grimace.

'Suddenly a terrible pain, here,' she gasped. 'Help me, Rose, I . . .'

Her eyes closed and she slumped against the table leg and slipped to the floor.

The house . . . Beth . . . the knife . . . What had the house done to Leonora? Rose began to panic, and then across her disordered thoughts she heard Ben's voice, very clear and crisp, giving her the instructions they had practised on the beach, with the mound of sand shaped like Mr Vingo.

Heart attack. All right, what do you do? Try to rouse the victim.

Leonora wouldn't wake, so Rose pulled her on to her back on the floor and knelt beside her in the white dress that was now crumpled and dirty from the moor.

Clear the airway. Listen and look for breathing. Rose tilted Leonora's head back so her tongue wouldn't block her throat, and put her cheek to her face. She felt no warm movement of air, saw no rise and fall of her chest.

What now? Pinch the nostrils so the air doesn't escape and give her four mouth-to-mouth breaths.

Practising with a towel over sand was one thing. Making a seal with your mouth over the cold, slack lips of someone you loved was another. Rose blew. Was it enough? Leonora

149

was wearing a skimpy sleeveless top. Rose easily saw her thin chest rise as the air went in.

What next? Feel for a pulse. She put her fingers on Leonora's neck where the carotid artery should be throbbing.

No pulse. Rose fought to control her panic. No pulse – Leonora was going to die. 'Don't die,' she begged her. 'You're not Beth. You don't have to die. You can't. Martin needs you. I won't let you die!' Somehow she had to start Leonora's heart beating. With an effort, she made herself remember what to do.

Kneeling above Leonora with one hand over the other on the bottom half of the breastbone, she began the pressure. One and – two and – three and . . . Fifteen times she pressed the heart between the breastbone and the backbone to make it pump. Then quickly back to Leonora's ashen face to tilt her head back and give her two more breaths, then back to press the heart fifteen more times under her hands.

A life in her hands. Oh God, don't let it be a death! She stopped just long enough to yell through the open door. 'Help me, somebody! Please – oh, somebody – help!' Then back to the rhythm of filling the lungs with air and forcing the heart to pump the blood up to the brain with the vital oxygen, without which the brain cells would rapidly die.

Every so often, Rose paused to shout for help and to feel for a pulse. Nobody heard her. There was no pulse. How long could she keep it up? Her shoulders and arms were aching. She was failing, failing. A great weight of doom was on her, as if all the unhappy spirits of this house were against her.

So *this* was the battle she was fighting for the horse. This was his crucial work: goodness and the joy of love against the evil of disaster and sorrow. If Leonora died, the battle was lost. The messenger of the grey horse had failed.

150

'It's no use,' Rose thought despairingly. 'It's too late. Why isn't someone else here? Why doesn't someone come? I can't do it.'

'You must,' said Favour in her thoughts, or was it Ben? 'Don't give it up . . . ever. Keep on for an hour. Two hours. You keep on and on. You're keeping the brain alive. you never give up.'

Rose drove herself to the effort, with her arms and back in pain and her own heart pounding. She kept on and on. Pausing to put her fingers on Leonora's slender neck, she felt the first flutterings of a pulse. It grew stronger – a beat, then a steady throb.

She'd done it! Two more mouth-to-mouth breaths, and as she lifted her head, she heard Leonora give a gasp, and then another. She was breathing. She began to open her eyes as feet clattered on the back step and Jim Fisher, in dungarees with a hammer in his hand, was in the room.

'What the –? I could have sworn I heard you shout, but Hilda said, "No, you're hearing things again, Jim," and I said, "No, listen Hilda," and I –'

'Get an ambulance quickly,' Rose said without looking up. 'Leonora. Leonora, look at me. It's all right. It's Rose. You're all right.'

She sat on the floor, supporting Leonora, as her breathing gradually became steady. 'It's all right,' she kept whispering. 'Everything's going to be all right.' But she wasn't only saying it to Leonora. She was saying it to the house and to the memory of all the unhappy, doomed people who had suffered here since the tragedy of Ronald and Beth. Her body was leaden with fatigue, but her mind was singing.

'I did it. I did it.'

'What you did . . .' Martin looked at her the next day very fondly. 'What you did can never be praised enough.'

151

'Oh, it was . . .' Rose couldn't quite say modestly, 'Oh, it was nothing,' because it wasn't. But she said, 'It was Ben's doing, really. He was the one who taught me what to do.'

'You were the one who saved Leonora's life.'

Some time after Leonora had been taken to the hospital in the ambulance, Martin had been brought home by Mr Selby from the farm, with his chair in the back of the truck.

'I was having a sleep in the sun,' Martin told Rose. 'Had a wonderful dream. I dreamed of legs. I used to do that, after the accident. I haven't had that dream for ages. I stood. I walked. And listen, Rose – I dreamed I rode a horse. When we galloped, it was like flying. When I woke up, you'd gone, so I got myself back as far as I could. Luckily the dog barked at me, and Mr Selby came out and gave me a lift home.'

Mr Selby was cross with her for leaving Martin alone on the moor, but Martin wasn't. He believed Rose when she told him, 'I just *knew* that something was wrong with Leonora. I had to come back. But please,' she added, 'tell them I came back to get your hat or something.'

'Why?'

'Well . . .' she blushed. 'They're all making a fuss of me. It's embarrassing. I don't want to make it worse by them thinking – you know – that I'm special, or anything.'

'You are, Rose. We'll never forget what you did.'

CHAPTER THIRTEEN

Rose knew that she would never forget any of it. If she lived for a hundred years, she would never forget that she had been the horse's faithful messenger, and had travelled with him through the winds of time to fight against evil and sorrow.

And win.

She had done it. If she hadn't taken all the journeys into the past with Favour, and followed up all the clues, right back to their source, she would not have been there with Lilian when Ronald made his tragic mistake, and she would not have heard Leonora calling for help, stricken as Beth had been stricken.

Leonora was saved, and the annexe house was saved. The haunting was gone for ever, Rose was sure of that. The sad, tormented ghosts of Ronald and Beth, who had destroyed so much in the lives of those who came after them, were finally laid to rest.

The front bedroom was . . . a bedroom. Nothing more; but a lot nicer than most hotel rooms you would find at the English seaside, or anywhere else.

The drooping chrysanthemum on the bedspread was the right way up again. How, in the laws of science, could it have been different? Rose was beginning to think she had imagined it.

The cupboard door stayed shut. When you opened it, as Rose did from time to time, to make sure, the dampness had gone completely, and, with it, the hint of the rotten sea smell, the legacy of the fisherman's jacket.

'Know what? That cupboard smells all right now,' she told her mother. 'Remember, it used to be so damp?'

'Well, the weather's changed. It's been dry for days.'

They were in the front garden, planting the two rose bushes that Rose had bought for her mother.

'But there's another thing about this house.' This was the best and most astonishing thing. 'You know that awful stain under the kitchen table?'

'The one that looked like spilled paint?'

The one that looked like spilled blood. Because it was blood, spilled a hundred years ago.

'All of a sudden, it's gone,' Rose said. 'How do you explain that?'

'Gloria must be using a new detergent. Oh Rose, I'm so glad we've got the annexe. We're making more money this year, and people love it. I think you do now, don't you? Remember how you turned against this house and imagined it was haunted?'

Mollie finished raking the earth round the roses, and stepped back to admire them, flowering a deep pink against the ivy-covered brick. 'This is a good house!' she proclaimed. 'Nothing bad could ever happen here.'

If I could only tell you.

Rose knew she never could. She could never tell anyone about the horse; not even Ben.

His big race was only a week away. She wrote to wish him luck:

I hope you win the championship. I hope you run marvellously.
Love from your Running Mate.
P.S. Thanks for teaching me resuscitation. You're right. It works.

There was still Mr Vingo.

The hotel was full for the weekend, and Rose did not get a chance to see him alone. He had to share his corner table

154

with two singers from the musical show that was playing at the theatre on Newcome Pier, but when Rose put down his plate of fried plaice and mashed and peas, he said without looking up, 'So you did it.'

'Oh – you know.'

'Of course.' He picked up his fork and cut through the golden breadcrumbs into the pure white flaky fish. 'You did well, Rose of all the world.'

After dinner, when Rose was in the garden putting the lawn chairs away, she heard music from Mr Vingo's room. The singers were upstairs, and he was playing the piano. They were singing a duet from the musical at the theatre. But below and through and above their voices, Mr Vingo began to play the tune, the piano rising up above the singing like a soaring bird.

Holding a chair, Rose stood with her mouth open, staring at the turret window.

Again? Now, when it was all over, and she had got used to the idea of being ordinary once more?

She dropped the chair and turned towards the wood, towards the moor, towards the valley.

This time, as she plunged down through the mist, there were no lurking shadowy figures. The mist parted into a shining path before her feet, and she ran straight down to the bridge and the swift flowing river.

The horse waited for her, his beautiful head turned towards the far distant huddle of white shacks at the end of the valley, where the tiny boats rode on the white-capped sea. Before, she had always shrunk back before his gaze, and glimpsed herself in his challenging eye very small and afraid. Now, as he turned his head, she stood up straight and looked full into his deep grey eye and saw herself mirrored there, erect and proud and confident.

Ready for his next command.

Ballad of Favour

A small child's cry of fear is the beginning of a new adventure for Rose Wood, chosen messenger of Favour, the magical Great Grey Horse.

What does it mean? Rose knows that when the horse carries her into different scenes and different times, she is supposed to find clues there.

'The child might have been abandoned – it might have been hurt,' she tells her friend Mr Vingo. 'But I don't know who it was or where it was or when it was.'

'Trust the horse,' says Mr Vingo. 'He'll show you.'

Centuries ago the horse belonged to the repulsive Lord of the Moor, and found fame in his heroic race to save a village. Now he lives on to fight against evil and despair.

As his messenger, Rose must fly with him to a small, decrepit, back street, and learn what makes the child cry so pitifully. The clues are there – a railway line, a fun fair, a TV programme, a birthday – but how do they fit together? Rose must find the solution before it is too late.

'JINNY' BOOKS
by Patricia Leitch

When Jinny Manders rescues Shantih, a chestnut Arab, from a cruel circus, her dreams of owning a horse of her own seem to come true. But Shantih is wild and unrideable.

This is an exciting and moving series of books about a very special relationship between a girl and a magnificent horse.

FOR LOVE OF A HORSE
A DEVIL TO RIDE
THE SUMMER RIDERS
NIGHT OF THE RED HORSE
GALLOP TO THE HILLS
HORSE IN A MILLION
THE MAGIC PONY
RIDE LIKE THE WIND
CHESTNUT GOLD
JUMP FOR THE MOON

Armada

BLACK HARVEST

by Ann Cheetham

A chilling story of terror and suspense...

The west coast of Ireland seems a perfect place for a family holiday — until everything begins to go horribly wrong...

Colin becomes aware of a ghastly stench from the land — a smell of death and decay... Prill is haunted by a fearsome skeleton-woman, who crawls through her dreams in hideous tormnt... Baby Alison falls sick with a sinister illness...

And their cousin Oliver? In those stiflingly hot summer days, as some nameless evil from the past closes in on them, Oliver remains unnaturally, unnervingly calm...

Armada

The Beggar's Curse
by Ann Cheetham

Is there no escape from the village of evil?

When Colin, Oliver and Prill arrive in Stang they realize
at once that something is wrong with the village. Up on
the surrounding hills spring is blossoming, but in this dark
little valley no flowers bloom and birds never sing.

Prill knows there is something sinister about the age-old
rituals of the village play. Colin knows the gruesome
incidents that keep happening are no accidents. But Oliver
alone knows the awful secret of Stang and sees the ancient
evil rising from the black waters of Blake's Pit. He feels
the terrible power of the beggarman's curse . . .

The Beggar's Curse is a chilling sequel to *Black Harvest,*
which was chosen in a special selection by British children
as one of their favourite books in 1984. One reader said of
it: "It was like opening a fridge door . . ."

Armada

Here are some of the most recent titles in our exciting fiction series:

☐ Pursuit of the Deadly Diamonds *J. J. Fortune* £1.25

☐ A Leader in the Chalet School *Elinor M. Brent-Dyer* £1.50

☐ Voyage of Terror *J. H. Brennan* £1.75

☐ The Witch Tree Symbol *Carolyn Keene* £1.50

☐ The Clue in the Broken Blade *Franklin W. Dixon* £1.25

☐ The Mystery of the Purple Pirate *William Arden* £1.25

☐ Chestnut Gold *Patricia Leitch* £1.25

☐ Monsters of the Marsh *David Tant* £1.75

Armadas are available in bookshops and newsagents, but can also be ordered by post.

HOW TO ORDER
ARMADA BOOKS, Cash Sales Dept., GPO Box 29, Douglas, Isle of Man, British Isles. Please send purchase price plus 15p per book (maximum postal charge £3.00). Customers outside the UK also send purchase price plus 15p per book. Cheque, postal or money order — no currency.

NAME (Block letters) _____

ADDRESS _____

_____

_____